The Old Man's Love Story

Chicana & Chicano Visions of the Américas

The Old Man's Love Story

Rudolfo Anaya

UNIVERSITY OF OKLAHOMA PRESS : NORMAN

Library of Congress Cataloging-in-Publication Data

Anaya, Rudolfo A.
The old man's love story / Rudolfo Anaya.
     pages cm— (Chicana & Chicano Visions of the Américas; Volume 12)
ISBN 978-0-8061-4357-6 (hardcover: alk. paper) 1. Older men—Fiction.
2. Loss (Psychology)—Fiction. 3. Marriage—Fiction. 4. Spiritual life—Fiction.
5. Grief—Fiction. 6. New Mexico—Fiction. I. Title.
PS3551.N27O43 2013
813'.54—dc23

                          2012046990

The Old Man's Love Story is Volume 12 in the Chicana & Chicano Visions of the Américas series.

The paper in this book meets the guidelines for permanence and durability of the Committee on Production Guidelines for Book Longevity of the Council on Library Resources, Inc. ∞

1 2 3 4 5 6 7 8 9 10

Contents

Preface and Acknowledgments

This book is my way of thanking family and friends whose kindness and love have sustained me these past few years. My wife's spirit has been constant, guiding and sheltering me. I pray daily to my ancestors who watch over me—so many guardian angels. I especially thank Belinda and Abe, who have been pillars of love and support.

In these stories, the old man struggles to understand the finality of death, and thus his search becomes a spiritual quest. Will he find the strength to go on living? What does he really believe about the afterlife? Will he find purpose in this new stage of life, or will grief consume him?

The old man's wife dies, but her spirit is still with him, and her essence lives in him. But if the life they once shared lives on only in fading memories, what happens when those memories die? There are so many questions about life and death that the old man needs to answer.

These stories are only a small part of the daily conversations the old man has with his wife. After the loss of a loved one, we realize that conversations with the departed never end. Love never ends.

The Old Man's Love Story

Oh, Lost

There was an old man who dwelt in the land of New Mexico, and he lost his wife. She died in his arms one night.

He sat at the side of her bed, held her fragile hands, pressed close to her, and listened to her barely beating heart.

"It's time to stop breathing," he whispered. "Tell your heart to stop. Your parents are waiting for you."

Beyond the veil waited those who had gone before. Her mother and father, her grandparents, his parents, friends.

"There," he said. "Take their hands."

She listened, smiled at him, took one last breath, and slipped away.

"We lost her," whispered the daughter who stood at the foot of the bed.

The old man nodded. Her spirit had flown, but even death could not diminish her loveliness. She had entered the night eternal as she had lived, gracefully.

A wind swept by, and she left the earth she loved so well— inevitable.

Her soul rose into a world of spirits, the realm of those departed. A universe of spirits, all the dead souls since time immemorial, a mourning wind that circled the earth.

These were the old man's thoughts as he caressed her face and whispered, "I will always love you . . ."

He didn't know just then that he was entering a time of grieving. He had found the strength to tell her it was time for her to leave, but now his thoughts troubled him. He remembered the words of a writer he admired: "Oh, lost and by the wind grieved. . . . Ghost, come home. . . ."

Gone. Yes.

"Where?" he asked, and turned toward a fluttering of wings in the room. Intimations of immortality, he thought.

He got up slowly, lit a candle, and placed it by her photograph. To light her way.

The house grew silent. Her daughters came and sat by her. Hushed telephone calls were made to family and friends. The attending nurse filled out forms.

His niece and her husband came and sat with the old man. Her grandchildren arrived, the old man's sisters and their husbands, nephews, nieces. All gathered to mourn her passage.

That night and into the early morning, they kept her wake. The wake for his wife was not planned, but the burning candle and guests made it feel right.

They sang, "Bendito, bendito, bendito sea Dios . . ." A song for her spirit, just like the people sang long ago. It consoled the old man's heart, and reminded him of velorios he had attended with his parents as a child.

Family and friends arrived to pray rosaries and alabados, kneeling by candlelight around the small, plain coffin. The kitchen bulged with food and drinks to sustain those who would pray until the sun rose.

Velorio, the word from vela, candle. Perhaps that's why he lit the candle right away. He remembered— light the way. Her presence in the room.

A week later they held a beautiful celebration of her life instead of a funeral. Those she had known commemorated her life, friends sang "Amazing Grace" and "Red River Valley." Later her ashes rested in an urn on the fireplace mantel. The old man moved into a new world, a deep silence.

At night he lay quiet in the bed they once shared, and he reached for her in the dark. Oh, lost.

Early one morning as the sun rose, he fed the dogs, then walked to the river. He called her name. The wind in the trees moaned, but did not answer. The river swept south, indifferent.

He walked in the neighborhood park and talked to her. He told her what he saw and felt.

"A lovely sky, the air is spring-fresh, look at those clouds . . ." He felt her nearby, next to him, in him.

In the small pond, a school of goldfish swam languidly. Ducks quacked. In the trees, birds sang. The world was moving on.

A couple passed by. He could tell they heard him talking to himself. He grew quiet, introspective.

An anguish deep in his soul sprouted and set loose suffocating tentacles. He had not cried since childhood, but now he cried. The loss he felt wracked his days and nights. He had entered a time of grieving, not knowing if it had an end.

He kept a journal recording his experiences of the sad season. He couldn't understand, or didn't want to accept, one of the most natural consequences of life: her death.

The old man had lived in the real world, he had tasted of the sacred and the profane, so why did he question life's mortality? A season of death comes to everyone. His parents, family members, friends— gone. He had felt the presence of death when those he loved had been laid to rest. What could he not accept?

He could not accept the finality of his wife's death. It wasn't fair. It didn't make sense.

Why? he asked. All those years together and now— empty space and silence.

Is she lost? Or am I the lost one? Why does the wind grieve as it sways the trees? Are those my cries I hear in the night? Are those my warm tears?

Love someone deeply, and the loss is insurmountable. They had been man and wife for many years, cleaving together. Now the sickle of death had severed the bond.

To ease the pain he told himself she was on a journey. She had entered the world of spirits. He would look for her in that world, communicate with her, find her.

He understood that everything in the world eventually dies. Even the earth is mortal. The pulse of life comes then passes away, touched by an eternal, universal spirit, God, the Great Mystery.

Life ends, like shining from shook foil.

He and his wife had lived an affirming life. A unity. They had been lovers in the bondage of mortality, and they would remain lovers even as death led them into the night eternal.

Grief became his journey, a new reality. Deep in his heart there was no consolation. Death's wound was too deep.

"Why? Why?" he asked over and over, but there was no answer in the silence.

The answer must lie in the world of spirits, he thought. I need to reach her.

What would he learn from his journey into the world of spirits? What illuminations might ease the pain in his soul? His search would parallel her journey, and at some point in infinity the two must meet.

He would find her.

The Photograph

The old man hired a woman to clean the house. While she worked he shut himself in his office, writing. His dogs, Oso and Chamisa, sat by him, sadness reflected in their eyes. The woman they loved had gone away. She had not returned.

The cleaning woman paused at the buffet and tossed the candle and wilted flowers into a wastebasket. She looked at the photograph. The man's wife. A beautiful face, but the lips were smudged, like someone had rubbed them with something. She placed the photograph in a drawer and went on with her work.

The old man picked up his cane, hobbled to his car, and drove to the store. For bananas. He didn't need much. Old people don't eat much, he thought.

You slow down, use a cane, then a wheelchair, finally a bed. The final passage. He knew.

"That's the way it is," he said to his wife.

That's the way it is, she answered.

He parked and looked around. I'm in the row by the tree with the dry branches. Looks withered. Needs water.

At the beginning of the century, his mother's parents had lived in the village of Puerto de Luna along the Pecos River. From that bloodline he had inherited a farmer's love of green.

He had grown up along the river, and years later he came to understand the river was sacred. As a boy he had felt the presence of the river, its soul, and he had lived fully in the mystery. The river gave and it took, the water flowed from time-past into his life, a time when he had run under the canopy of huge cottonwood trees, feeling the hot sand beneath his feet, becoming one with the nature of the river. When the river ran low, playas formed, sandbars deposited by previous floods. He and his friends would run to the playas and dive into the water.

People hurried in and out of the store. The old man took a grocery cart and leaned into it. He went slowly, pausing at the liquor aisle. He studied the prices for a long time, finally putting a bottle of cheap vodka in the cart.

Sip it with orange juice, he thought.

For pain, he had often told his wife. It's either that or take the medications.

Yes, she said. She understood.

Afternoons they had sat on the porch looking out at the garden. The hollyhocks were blooming. He always had a drink before dinner. Good tequila when the Social Security check arrived at end of the month.

Sometimes he drank two. Deadens the pain, he liked to say.

She didn't drink, but she knew about pain.

At bedtime he took his medications. To sleep.

Used to be sex, he'd say as he got in bed.

Used to be, she'd smile and lay softly beside him.

Once a woman, twice a child, he said.

Yes, she agreed. Once a man, twice a child. They'd laughed softly in the dark night.

He paid for the vodka, orange juice, and two bananas.

"Don't buy green bananas," he joked with the young clerk. She smiled. She didn't have the slightest idea what he meant, but she was pretty and he couldn't help but glance at her cleavage. Ah, he thought, even old men like to look at soft curves. They think we forget about a woman's beauty.

A flickering memory suddenly burned bright. His wife's lovely breasts. Other memories came piling on him. Whenever he passed down the cereal aisle, tears filled his eyes. He would never again buy her favorite cereal.

Everything contained a memory. Where could he hide? He touched his eyes with his shirtsleeve. He hated to cry in public. Damn!

Memories clog the mind, he thought. He realized he was forgetting names. Strange how he could remember every character and twist and turn in the novel he was writing, but forget the names of former colleagues, even friends. Selective memory, he guessed.

Memories appeared to push out the present. Be damned if I forget my Social Security number, he thought. Be double-damned if they take away my driver's license.

The car and his memories were all that remained of freedom. Thoughts that rambled through his mind seemed to be like time travel. Images of the past were a kind of freedom from whatever was real in the world.

He believed less and less in reality. Reality was fading. He thought it was all a mystery anyway. Could he trust memories? After all, what was a memory? A sudden explosion in brain cells, an awareness, remembrances of times past? Illusive. Was there any substance in the world?

The beauty of the earth and its firmament were a mystery to be enjoyed. He lived and breathed in the Great Mystery, and it, too, was momentary, fleeting.

A driver full of road rage whizzed by and yelled, "Use it or lose it, old man!"

"Screw you!" the old man shouted in defiance.

He had to remind himself to drive slowly. Give the crazies plenty of room. If he drove slowly, they honked. If he drove fast, they gave him one-finger salutes.

An old man couldn't win. You get old and what do you get? A little more grouchy and deeper in debt.

Best to be home. Home was safe. Maybe?

Old people fall. In bathrooms, on stairs. One friend had fallen off the toilet. Damn. Break a hip bone and you might as well hang up the tennis shoes.

He constantly had reminded his wife, go slow. She reminded him, go slow. Old people fall. They all did at one time or another. His wife had fallen. He felt he hadn't been there for her. Her time at the rehabilitation center had been dreadful. She had called him constantly, begging him to get her out. Looking back, he had known it was the beginning of the end.

Most memories were like scenes in a movie. So many good times, simple times, intimate times. But also sad memories that brought tears.

"Lovers Forever," he had written on a Valentine's Day card. A magnet held it on the refrigerator door.

Her smile was worth a thousand Valentines.

Sometimes a memory surfaced as guilt.

Any regrets? he had asked her once.

No regrets, she had told him.

Her understanding had brought tears to his eyes. She had faced life head-on. Two strong women had shaped his life: his wife and his mother. For that he gave thanks.

He was breathing hard by the time he entered the kitchen. The dogs greeted him with excitement. Always waiting for him to return, always happy.

"Even getting out of the car is difficult," he said. "Didn't used to be."

They had often joked about what used to be. Nothing was like it used to be. They knew.

He paused. Someone had been in the house. He sensed a presence. "Who?" he asked. The dogs barked. Yes, someone was here!

The old man dropped the grocery bag on the table and hurried to the buffet where he kept her photograph. He always kissed the photo when he left the house and when he returned. During the day when he passed by the buffet he would stop, talk to her, and kiss her picture. She was in the photo. She could hear him.

"Mi querida, mi preciosa," he whispered. My Beloved, precious.

Mihita. He didn't remember when he started calling her his daughter. His father had called his mother mihita.

The photograph was gone! He felt a sharp pain in his chest.

What the hell!

The flowers were gone, and the candle, too. He looked around. How could it be? Things just don't disappear. Or do they? Am I losing it? Of course he was.

He felt the panic rise in him. Where did she go?

Maybe I moved the picture. That's it! I moved it! But where? He had forgotten.

He kept her wedding dress in a downstairs closet. Daily he went to the closet and looked in the large box. To remember. To smell the lingering fragrances. Dry and brittle now.

He threw his cane aside and hurried downstairs. Maybe I put her picture in the closet. Need to find it! She's calling me! Need to find it!

The old man tripped on a stair tread and fell hard. Later, he opened his eyes and heard the dogs whimpering, felt them licking his face.

"I have to find the photograph," he said. She was in it! Her spirit lived in the picture! Her shining eyes.

That night images of clouds filled his dreams.

Old Men Need Kisses, Too

Once in a while the need surfaced. He didn't know if he could trust his emotions. He felt the need to be close to a woman. Was it desire? A strange yearning? Or loneliness?

Damn! Blood's too old for desire, he thought. Blood gets old and it dries up, clogs, leads to heart attacks, strokes. Doesn't flow to the right places anymore. Dissolution.

He tried to stop thinking. No one wants to hear an old man's problems.

I do, she whispered. She would understand what was bothering him. She always knew.

You get old and what do you get, a little more scrawny and deeper in debt. It's a young man's world. You had your turn, chango. Is that what he had become? A monkey man. Walking around like a chimp on its knuckles. Dragging his lame leg.

The accidents of youth caught up with the old. Arthritis settled in old fractures, nerves and bones ossified, joints needed oiling. Either that or replacement.

The heart. Oh, the heart. Blood so clogged that desire could no longer move along the arteries. Venus, the goddess of love, deserted the veins.

Be still, my heart.

Was he feeling the last gasp of sex hormones in the blood? An atavistic need?

How can I explain this need? he asked himself in the dark of night. It doesn't seem right thinking about another woman.

She was curled next to him, so close he felt her warmth.

There's a Room of Loneliness, she said.

He nodded. He lived in that room a lot lately.

When they first met she had carved rooms in his heart. They were in love. She had built beautiful chambers in his heart and named them.

Here is the Room for Making Love, she told him. He felt he had died and gone to heaven when he entered that room.

Here a Room for Sleeping. In winter her warmth had comforted his sleep. In summer they'd enjoyed cool breezes flowing through the open window and the drone of crickets. Moonlight sliding off shining green leaves. Her moon, her cycles.

Each passage of the moon requires its own kind of love, she told him. She watched the moon as it grew then ebbed, knew the names of ancient moon goddesses.

She built a Room of Fragrances where her cologne and lipstick blended with her body's aromas. She had loved tanning in the morning sun, her sweat a fragrance from foreign, exotic blossoms. He breathed deep. Ecstasy.

Love was a luxury. Free. God gave the gift to all who lived in the natural world. He had taken it and been fulfilled.

She built a large Room for Reading. They had read constantly, religiously. Bulging bookshelves throughout their home held their treasures. Even the car contained their books. There gnawed at their souls a hunger for life, a thirst for knowledge.

A Room for Travel where they plotted trips to foreign countries. So we take out a loan. Better do it now! Why wait?

They didn't wait, they went, and now images of their adventures filtered through his mind, kaleidoscopic scenes. There was no end to those variegated places, now here, now there, now everywhere. He remembered streets in Paris, the morning mist at Stonehenge, the pyramids of Giza, the Parthenon, Mexico. Especially Mexico.

Daily and nightly, year after year, she led him into the rooms she had built. A sense of wonder filled him when he explored the chambers of his heart. Overwhelming joy. Love was constantly a new adventure, a learning, a going deep into body and spirit.

She opened doors and in poured joy and sunshine. Her kisses

were like a cool breeze on a warm day. Sensations close to orgasms.

I was pretty dumb, huh?

Yes, she murmured.

You don't have to agree!

She smiled and closed the door to the Room for Sleeping. It was time to rest.

He thought he could hear her breathing. The soft rhythms of the breath of life, in and out, coming and going, starting and stopping.

There was one room he was not supposed to enter. She had called it her Room of Secrets.

Room of my past, she said. No need to go there.

But I've told you everything about my past, he argued.

Yes, she said, but the past is filtered by the conscience of he who tells it, so it is an illusion. Even in the greatest love stories there are secrets. And secrets are best kept in a locked room.

Okay. I agree. Maybe I didn't tell you everything. For one thing, I had plenty of girlfriends when I was young.

I know, she said.

Damn! What didn't she know?

You are my love story, he said.

As long as you remember, love is constant.

I will always remember, he said.

Her breath held the fragrance of lilacs wafting through the open window. Spring had arrived and the garden he had cultivated for her was blooming.

I'm lonely, he found the courage to say. He didn't want to concern her with his loneliness. I miss you so much— I just feel I need someone to touch.

I know, she said.

You know?

Yes. All your stories tell that we need the human touch.

She remembered all the stories he had written. But now he couldn't touch her, couldn't hold her. Was she, too, lonely in the world of spirits?

I kiss your photograph every day— He felt a lump in his throat.

His loneliness was palpable. What could she do?

Anyway, he said, who would want to kiss an old man? They think we smell. I shower! I shave! I use deodorant! He paused. My body feels dry and crinkly. I don't sweat like I used to. I can go days without a bath.

You're on a new plane now, she said.

They had lived their lives by constantly moving on to new planes, levels of love, epiphanies, consciousness, knowledge, dreams. Sloughing off old, useless ways of being, not afraid of new experiences. Like snakes shedding old skins and glistening anew. Excitement for life, the miracle they explored together.

Now he was alone.

A dried-out plane, he scoffed.

That's not like you, she said.

It's true. Is the senior citizen center supposed to be my new life? I don't like it! Some of the men *do* smell— one even wets his pants. He won't wear those Depends diapers. The old wags smell too— use a lot of cheap perfumes.

"We all smell!" he blurted out. "So what!" His words echoed in the dark.

She drew close, her shadow a comforting blanket, as it had always been. She knew what was bothering him. The loneliness was wearing him down.

I use Bengay on my knees. Women don't like the smell of Bengay!

She moaned, a sorrowful sound. She felt his loneliness, but what could she do?

"A woman's body to hold— you know?"

She knew.

There is a Room of Kisses, she said. They had shared that communion, sacred as the taking of the Eucharist.

Everyone needs kisses.

Even old men?

Yes, even old men.

Me?

Yes, you. The door to the Room of Kisses is open— don't close it.

Ah, she understood. She always had. I'll shower tomorrow, he resolved. Shave. Go to the senior citizen center. Maybe one of the gray-haired ladies might want to tango.

No, he corrected himself. The old gals there didn't seem kissable. Or were they? Did they also feel the yearning he felt? Was he thinking only of himself and forgetting that a kiss is a two-way street? Intimacy in that erogenous zone of lips, teeth, and tongue.

Your kisses always excited me, he whispered in the dark.

We were made for each other, she said.

The night was restless. A wind blew in from the east, carrying away the lilac's perfume. Lilac bushes blooming in the garden. Heart-shaped leaves. Whitman's trinity, the death of Lincoln.

Love, grief, and memory. The sad, symbolic world of three, the old man's trinity.

He felt as restless as the night. Could any woman ever kiss him the way she had? Why the nagging need? A yearning? Call it whatever. He had been alone over a year; he knew loneliness.

Is there a Room of Yearning? he asked.

Of course, she answered. I filled it every day.

I know. It's just that I'm stupid. Tonto!

Go with the feeling, she said.

Go with the feeling?

Yes.

He started humming. Poor ol' Kaw-Liga. The Hank Williams song about the wooden Indian who never got a kiss. Poor ol' Kaw-Liga, he never got a kiss . . . poor ol' Kaw-Liga, he don' know what he miss. The wooden Indian standing by the door. It was a song from his childhood. Came from a radio station somewhere in Texas. Country music. The people from his hometown listened to those songs, and Mexican corridos, ballads that told of lost love.

He hummed and memories sprouted, like clouds from the distant past. He thought of the people from the eastern New Mexico llano, hard-working paisanos who had settled along the Pecos River Valley. His people. He had written their story.

No television in those days, only radio. Late at night on the lonely plains they heard Hank singing Kaw-Liga's lonely lament. Could life be lived without kisses? the people wondered.

I'm thirsty, he said.

Need a drink?

No. He wasn't thirsty for water. It was something else. Her kisses. But that was over and done with. He could kiss her photograph, but she couldn't kiss back. The photograph was like the urn that held her ashes. Silent and dark.

Her image was as lovely as ever, but more and more he realized she could not kiss him.

Like you used to, he said.

Nothing is like it used to be, she whispered.

Yeah, he agreed.

The wind was rising, funneling through Tijeras Canyon into the city, blowing Alburquerque dreams away.

Tanto tiempo disfrutando de tu amor, he hummed. Yo no sé si tenga fin la eternidad. He couldn't remember the words, but he could hum the melody. Sabor a mi. I still taste you.

Not even eternity could erase the taste of her kisses.

Is there a room called the Taste of Kisses? he asked.

Yes, she answered. You know that.

Yes. He smiled. He felt her in his heart. Curled up snug as a bug.

You're snug as a bug, he said. He loved to tease her.

Yes, she murmured, a Snug as a Bug Room.

Gotta go, he said.

Pee?

No. Close the window.

He got up slowly. Go slow, they always told each other. Especially after she had taken the bad fall. Go slow.

He went to the window and looked out. The wind blew through the Sandia Mountains canyon into the Rio Grande Valley. Those sleeping did not hear the wind, but the old man heard its songs. He breathed deep. The wind carried the taste of llano rain— it had rained in Kaw-Liga's country. The rain kissing the earth. Perhaps there was hope.

He gathered the nerve to ask, What do you think? This feeling I have about a woman.

From desire springs hope, she whispered. I want joy to return to your heart. The Room of Loneliness is not forever.

He smiled and closed the window. Perhaps the wind would not blow everything away.

Hope? With hope, one could learn to dream again.

The Gym

Ernesto wore a Speedo. His thing bulged. Every morning he came strutting down to the pool. The old men and women doing water aerobics paused. Their instructor, a thin, young blonde, turned to greet Ernesto.

This happened every morning. The older women glanced at each other. Their looks said show-off.

One heavy-set woman smiled at Ernesto. From her place at the pool's edge she could look up at him. She picked that spot every day.

The old man shook his head and continued moving his arms, up and down and across. Buoyed by water was a sure way to build muscle tone without using weights. Besides, the weight room was full of jocks. Muscle-builders. Steroid factories.

There was no love in the weight room, only competitive glares. My abs can beat your abs.

Better here, the old man thought. In the water, returning to my fish nature. Besides, he enjoyed the women. A couple were not bad at all. One drawback, the chlorine that stung his eyes.

The old man glanced at the heavy-set woman staring at Ernesto. He guessed stout women were lonelier than most. It wasn't a truth he would bet on, just a feeling.

I'm certainly not going around saying fat women are lonely, he thought. Keep it to myself. Besides, the country was obese, so that meant it was lonely. Fat and lonely Americans.

The old man did occasionally glance at the way the women's breasts swayed in the water. Comes from time spent nursing, he thought. To a baby, momma's breasts appeared gigantic, warm, nurturing.

He thought of his wife's lovely breasts. Just right. How many nights had he pressed his head against her and fallen asleep? The thought made him sad. So much about her he missed.

It was like that. Memories made one lonely. Maybe the whole world was lonely. Memories appeared when one least expected, and everybody had memories. Was everyone sad?

Some women in the pool looked sad. They laughed the loudest. The old man knew. Some said laughter was the best medicine. Laughter was also a cover-up.

"Chlorine," he mumbled, wiping his eyes.

Everyone has a handicap. A feeling of not being like others. Inadequate.

Ernesto was talking to the aerobics instructor. He turned to make sure everyone admired the bulge in his Speedo. Swimming trunks that looked like bikini bottoms. Speedos were popular for men under thirty. Boys.

Let them, the old man thought. How many times did I show off when I was young? He couldn't remember. Bragging about conquests was part of being young. Sex seemed to rule the young. So much identity tied up in hormones, Mother Nature's insistence.

On top of that I had a lot of Catholic guilt, the old man thought. The desires of the body were sinful. Damn, I don't know how I survived.

His potential had blossomed with his wife's love. He began to forget the escapades of his youth. The faces of young women he had romanced disappeared into a pool of memories.

Sooner or later everything disappeared into memory, a lake of dark water. Once in a while bubbles rose from the depths and exploded on the surface, consciousness. Oh, yeah. I remember. What was her name?

The aerobics class grew restless. The water, softly lapping against the sides of the pool, made a sucking sound. Like making love. The juices of the men and women spilled into the water. Sperm darted momentarily, seeking ovum's safe harbor before the chlorine killed the microscopic cells.

The women whispered to each other.

The old man looked at Vicki, moving her arms in the water, smiling. She was kind. She often greeted him. Some days she waited, took his hand, and helped him down the stairs. She'd had polio as a kid.

Maybe I could make it with Vicki, he thought.

The aerobics are good for you, his wife replied.

Not a jealous bone in her. She knew him too well.

Every day, he would walk to the park, and every day he would describe for her what he saw. He felt her beside him. When he returned home he would go to her photograph.

"Look at you, smiling." He would kiss the photograph, imagine that she kissed back, that he could smell her fragrance. He would say sweet words to her in Spanish, "Querida. Preciosa. You look lovely. Spring is in the air. The goldfish in the pond are swarming, making goldfish love. The swallows have returned, the ducks, too, are making love. Did you know ducks are monogamous? And the heron is back. Spring clouds cavorting in a clear blue New Mexican sky."

When a man is feeling good, even clouds make love.

Now all was present tense. He'd point out things and speak to her as his life unfolded. She was with him, in him. So if he had the hots for Vicki, she was sure to know.

She had not gone away. Maybe the flesh he had loved so well now lay silent in the urn, ashes, a reminder, something symbolic, but not her. Not her essence.

The old man began to understand that those one loved dearly don't disappear. They're like breath— here, aware. A kind of resurrection he needed to understand.

"Hey, old man," Ernesto called from the edge of the pool. "How's it hanging?"

The old man didn't answer. He didn't want to be friends with Ernesto. He didn't like Ernesto. Ernesto was a bully. Oh, he never hit or pushed anyone. He was loud and friendly. He just wanted everyone to look at him. In the shower room Ernesto took off his Speedo and turned to make sure the men noticed he used a special shampoo.

"Got to take care of what pleases the ladies," he said every day. The men shook their heads and left the shower room.

"How's it hanging?" Ernesto repeated, laughing.

That's how he bullied. With his thing. It irritated the hell out of the old man.

You grow old and everything shrinks, the old man thought as he was driving home. Speeding. He guessed he was angry at himself.

Go slow, his wife whispered.

"But he's a fake! A bully!"

Sizes are overrated, she said. Love is two persons becoming one.

The old man slowed down. She was right. She knew how to calm him.

Don't be angry, she cautioned. Anger only stresses you, not the person who causes the anger.

You built rooms in my heart, the old man retorted. So there's a Room of Anger.

Yes, she replied. I made many rooms in your heart, but you had your own rooms before I came. You are who you are.

Why are some rooms dark? Like a haunting.

Our human bondage, our inheritance, she replied. You know.

The old man stopped at a light. "Yes," he said. He knew.

A Room of Anger, Room of Envy, Room of Spite, Room of Hate, Room of War and Killing, Room of Bloody Conquest . . . they're all there. In the heart, in the blood.

The country was at war in the Fertile Crescent while in Africa children starved.

She's right, he thought. We inherit all that bad stuff. Part of our nature. In the DNA, they say. Even the pope can't erase the rooms that cause so much suffering and grief. They're old as humanity.

He breathed a sigh of relief.

"Thank you," he whispered, "for the Room of Love."

De nada, she replied. She was smiling. Drive slow.

"I will," he said.

He stopped and bought a bouquet of flowers to place next to her photograph. When he got home he sat in the swing shaded by grape vines while the dogs explored the garden and then came to sit by him. He drank a beer. Water aerobics always tired him.

He dozed off. She opened the door to the Room of Love, took his hand, and they walked down the beach at Mazatlán. They lay side by side on the warm sand. She covered him with suntan lotion, caressing him softly.

Eros was the gift God gave humans. Life was destined to be damn painful, so God gave man and woman zones of pleasure. Kissing and caressing awakened the body, nerves tingled, moans of love were drowned by sea-foam slapping against the sand.

On the beach the vendors called, advertising their wares to the tourists. Sandals! Straw hats! Serapes! Your name on a grain of rice. Free margaritas with a coupon. Just for you, my friend. Real silver from Taxco. Almost free! Want to go fishing?

Life on the beach was as near as they ever got to heaven.

He didn't return to the water aerobics class. Weeks later Vicki called to tell him, Ernesto was dead.

"What? How?"

"He dove into the pool like he always did. Showing off, splashing us."

"He drowned?"

"Well, not really. We dragged him out of the pool. It was his heart, someone said later. He was taking loads of male enhancement drugs and steroids. Taking care of . . . you know."

Yes, the old man knew.

"There's a rosary tonight. I can pick you up."

"Yes. Thanks." He smiled. Would they bury Ernesto in his Speedo?

Siesta Time

She opened the door to the Room of Loneliness. He was sitting in the rocking chair, napping.

They had been teachers, and during summer breaks they had enjoyed the mornings, tanning a rich brown as they gardened, then resting after lunch. Love flourished in the afternoons. At home, at their mountain cabin, in every country they visited, in Mexico—especially Mexico.

He had written: The ancient gods created Mexico because they loved the mexicanos, and so love flourished in that dynamic earth. The indigenous people honored the Lord and Lady of Duality, givers of life, male/female all wrapped into one.

When man and woman become one, love blossoms, it explodes. Poets struggle to describe the moment when time stands still. Few succeed.

Ancient tribes from Alaska to Tierra del Fuego made warfare to be sure, and anthropologists never tired of writing about those conflicts. But scholars often forgot that every tribe's Way of Knowledge was infused with love and respect for the earth and all natural things.

Of nature's creatures, woman was most held in awe. She propagated the earth. Her birth and death mysteries described the ebb and flow of seasons, cycles of the moon, revolutions of the planet Venus. Woman was created in the image of the earth: big breasts, rotund stomach where rested Eve's belly button, wide hips, fruit-bearing womb. Like la madre tierra, round not flat.

Centuries ago, Spanish-speakers from Mexico had arrived in New Mexico, where now dwelt the old man. Españoles mexicanos.

Iberians born in Mexico who mixed it up with the Native people, thus giving birth to mestizos, a New World people.

Let the bloodlines be mixed without shame, the old man wrote.

The Europeans searched for gold, only to be met by Natives who handed them ears of corn.

See, it is like this, the Natives said, corn, squash, chile, beans. Meat from our four-legged brothers. It is like this.

Those ancestors learned to love the earth and its bounty.

The old man and his wife had traveled throughout Mexico, the country they loved most. Hand in hand they walked among the many archeological sites, climbed the Pyramid of the Sun and the Pyramid of the Moon, breathed the air, listened to Aztec drums, songs of departed warriors, and bowed to the miracle of la Virgen de Guadalupe. The goddess reigned supreme in every baroque church they visited, she who once ruled as Tonantzín at ancient sites.

We loved Mexico.

Yes, she answered. Cuernavaca and Ana's home, San Miguelito.

Years ago he had taught a summer seminar on Chicano literature at a university in Mexico City. He and his wife stayed with Ana, who had recently been widowed, and in the following weeks a close family relationship evolved. Thereafter they visited her every summer, spending most of the time in her finca in Cuernavaca.

It was the place to be when we were young . . .

Oh, yes, she agreed.

In Mexico the mythical mother was Cihuacóatl, consort of Quetzalcóatl. Her massive stone sculpture rests in the anthropology museum in Mexico City. Remember?

Of course, she replied. We spent hours admiring her.

Well, a scholar recently unlocked the cosmological secrets of the sculpture. Aztec religion and creative imagination revealed for all to understand. What an incredible and fascinating past that country has.

And we touched part of it. Go on.

The legend says Quetzalcóatl retrieved the bones of the dead from Mictlán, land of the dead. Cihuacóatl ground them in a precious jade vessel. Quetzalcóatl bled his penis on the bones, and man and woman were brought back to life.

Life-giving, she said.

They had spent many summers at Ana's finca. Later they named their cabin in the Jemez Mountains after her San Miguelito— a San Miguelito del Norte.

Afternoons in Cuernavaca were for loving. Especially during the rainy season. The music of the gods, a heavy Mexican rain pounding the roof tiles, thunder bolts exploding. The orgasms of the ancient volcanoes, Popo and Itza, made the earth shake.

Yes, Mexico was for loving. Without passion there is no Mexico. Without passion there are no telenovelas.

In Mexico they had come to a new awareness of their natural state. A new plane, bonding flesh and soul, a deeper fulfillment of their love.

The vegetables and fruits from Mexico are primal and exotic, he told her. Each displays the eroticism of earth, sun, and rain. The sweet juices of corn are the juices of the woman, the fiery chiles the heat of the man. Mango snacks after love. A split papaya exposes seeds like a woman's ripe ovaries.

She smiled. Quite a sexy theory. They laughed.

Nature rules the instincts of soul and flesh. Earth, sun, and rain give birth, as do eruptions of fire from volcanoes. The sun of Mexico is erotic— oh, it can be killing to be sure. If you're a campesino with your corn field burning up, you pray for rain, not for sun.

On the Mazatlán beach they soaked up the morning sun, and for sure there was going to be some loving.

Life is difficult for the poor, she said. She knew.

Poor Mexico, so far from God and so near the United States.

She loved the Mexican people. Maybe that's why she came into his life, she Anglo and he a nuevo mexicano. Will the marriage last, family wondered.

They don't know the depth of our love, she had answered.

She had two daughters from a previous marriage, and although he would never truly be their new father, the family thrived because her love for them held them together. And my love for her, he thought. A love fired in a celestial forge.

She read poetry on Ana's terraza overlooking the jardín and the pool. He had been writing a story about a jardinero.

Others find timidity in the people, she said. I find open hearts, acceptance, love. All should come to Mexico and learn such goodness.

Yes, she loved the mexicano soul, admired the people, understood their evolution.

Afternoons on the beach at Mazatlán, the sea slopping against the receptive sand, her life-pulsing cry. Orgasms were communion with her goddess. Such was the ecstasy of those days.

Now, even in the midst of his dream in the rocking chair, he sensed a wave of sadness pass over her. She could feel his sorrow and worried that he spent too much time in his Room of Loneliness.

He knew she wanted to take his hand and draw him out.

Where?

To life. There are others who love you. Family. Friends. Take time away from the novel; it's consuming you. Get out of the house sometimes— then she hesitated. I can't create your purpose now. You are a man of visions. Characters appear from the recesses of your imagination and you always feel compelled to write their stories. Now you are writing your own passage through grief.

It was true he favored the Room of Loneliness. Her absence had created a vacuum. His sadness would make or break him.

She couldn't touch him. She had become a memory. That's all that was left in the end, memories.

Remember?

Yes.

Years ago, whenever he returned from the gym he would drink a beer and watch the *Jerry Springer Show* on TV, laughing. It's slapstick, he'd said. Remember the Three Stooges?

They always talked during lunch— about comedy and tragedy, favorite plays and books, movies, politics, friends and family, travel, a multitude of things. Now those conversations had become wisps of memory.

I'm forgetting the times we made love.

Too many to remember, she said.

He laughed. I remember some . . .

Memory is selective. What we don't need gets pushed to the back.

And pain? he asked. Why?

Because we're human. There's always been pain.

Now it's bending me earthward, he said. Spiraling down. The doctor says he wants to preserve my quality of life. I have trouble peeing. Prostate, the doc says. I walk bent over, arthritis, weakness, depression, maybe I'm drinking too much.

She sighed and reached for him. We didn't know getting old would be like this, she said.

Nobody told us.

Did we really understand what our parents went through in their old age?

Lord forgive us.

She looked at him, worried. He needs to know I'm well. My wandering is over. I'm with him.

He believed her soul was in the world of spirits, an afterlife animated by spirits.

God is everywhere, he thought. His bones are stuck in the earth. He needed to believe.

His ancestors had died and become saints. His parents were saints in the world of spirits. He asked them to take care of his Beloved. He asked a blessing for his dead brothers and sisters. Each morning his prayers went on and on, asking a blessing for everyone.

Go to them, he had told her the night she had taken her last breath. Take the hands of your father and mother. Visit my parents. They wait.

Now he wasn't sure. He was in turmoil.

The universe was breathing, conscious, alive. Once soul is cast in flesh it has no end, it has no beginning, maybe always was. Could he hold on to this truth?

How I enjoyed our conversations. What we learned, what we shared. Searching for the deeper meaning of life . . . Our time was not wasted.

Afternoons on the beach, they would hear the last calls of the vendors as they headed home. The sea grew sluggish, like a kiss just before falling asleep. Kids shouting, parents calling.

So many books, so much time discussing life lived fully, then life's aftermath. They arrived at a simple truth— death is inevitable. Now for him, simple was complex.

She knew his mind. He must know I am well. He prays that his saints guide me. I, too, am a saint, and he asks me to watch over him. "Mi angelito," he whispers. "Help me. What am I to do? Am I doing the right thing? Rub my aching back like you used to" . . . So much to ask of the departed.

I have become his guardian angel.

She reached out to touch his shoulder. Something she had not done since her departure. Something she yearned to do, if yearning was the emotion she felt. Or was it loneliness? Am I, too, lonely? she wondered.

She didn't want him to think loneliness existed in her world. But there it was, in her heart, touching her lightly as a dove's feather, a sigh.

The complexity of the whole shebang didn't end with the last breath of life. Of what can we be sure?

Everything becomes a memory, he whispered.

He felt her nearby, opened his eyes, and reached out, hands trembling.

"Are you here?"

In the garden honeybees buzzed the blooming hollyhocks. A dove alighted on the fence.

It's her, he thought. Taken a new form. Come to reassure me.

"Hijita!" he called. "You came home!"

The dogs jumped up. Why had the master called? No one in the yard. Only a dove on the fence.

"Bendito sea Dios," he said. "Was I dreaming? Is it you?"

The dove coo-cooed, a soft cry of love.

"Remember Cuernavaca? Remember the beach at Mazatlán?"

He listened intently for an answer. Again the dove sang. The old man smiled. Of course she remembers. There is no wall of separation between life and death. Soul mates mean two souls have become one.

"Thank you for coming, " he whispered.

I was always here, she replied. I live in you as you live in me. Love is a dream, and in that dream lovers lie together on a bed of clouds. Love never ends, it never dies.

The Journal

The old man kept a journal, a record of his emotional roller coaster ride.

He kept up with the political struggles of the time and listened daily to commentators on the nation's state of affairs. Religion had entered politics, crazy notions like "my God is better than yours" prevailed. It seemed a kind of mass hysteria had affected the country. Greed had devastated the economy, and millions had lost homes and meager savings.

In Sudan, Uganda, and Somalia, millions of children were starving. The old man bowed his head and prayed. He lived in reality, and reality smelled really bad.

Maybe I need to talk to someone, he thought.

He didn't want to go around with his heart on his sleeve. He kept the crying jags to himself, sitting in his bedroom or in the swing under the grape vines. He stayed busy, writing, calling a few friends, home maintenance. The world didn't need his raw emotions. The real victims were the starving children and the dispossessed.

He was learning that the world quickly moved on. It didn't stop for those in mourning. Time on earth was brief.

Time seemed to stream into a gigantic memory, and it moved fast, evaporating everything in its path. Time did not wait, time did not stop.

Once upon a time, making love stopped time for a few, explosive, god-like seconds. Could he find such love again? Was it possible? At forty or fifty maybe, but not for an old man.

So the old man moved on. He made a list of his reality:

A drought had pressed down on the land he loved. He worried for farmers who were losing crops and livestock. Drought also in Africa, in Mexico, and in the land he loved and lived in, the Greater Southwest.

Conservation of water. Use as little as possible in the garden, washing dishes, bathing— take a shower with someone you like. The old man laughed. Yeah, right.

He prayed the politicians would get things right for the country, not just for the wealthy and powerful. Take care of the 90 percent. Finally a promising movement was sweeping across the country, with young people involved like in the '60s. Hope in the air.

The faces of starving children made him wince and pray. What to do? Who to curse?

Wars in Iraq and Afghanistan. The young dying. So much pain in the world . . . why? The age-old question: Why does God allow suffering?

On and on his list went. The recession, the unemployed, people losing their homes, global economic change, savings accounts lost, electronic books managed by corporations that cared only about the bottom line, birthdays, letters to write, back pain . . .

What was the public thinking? The nation? Who controlled the realities of the day?

The old man wrote: I have always been involved in life, I'm no wallflower. I still do some things. Water tomato plants, get the oil changed, go with a friend to our hometown for our fifty-second high school reunion, drive to the cabin, check on the apple trees, buy presents, check my 401k, worry about my bank balance running low, review a friend's book, watch telenovelas . . .

But something was missing in his life. So he called his lady friend he met at the class reunion. She had lost her husband a few years back. Widows and widowers found each other. Like dolphins lost in the Sargasso Sea, their sad vibes drew them together. Love in the time of the nursing home. Could a night under a woman's sheets cure loneliness? Of course not. He needed something more substantial . . . what?

He liked his lady friend, felt something was beginning to work. Brief sparks of joy flared. Spontaneous joy.

You understand, he said to his wife, why I'm writing this journal.

Yes, she answered. A record of your journey. What you experience and discover.

A grief counselor suggested I keep a journal. If you can't talk to people at least write what you feel. Conquer grief.

Grief is personal, he wrote. Best keep it to myself. Maybe share it with a couple of old friends who had recently lost their wives. They talked on the phone, but in the end, each went his own way. Snippets of sharing, and always the complaint— night is the hardest.

Time will heal. A cliché. Sharing emotions didn't come easy. Best write about reality.

But so little seems real, he wrote. Some days don't make sense. Why am I still here? Feel like I'm walking in a fog, stumbling. One false step and I disappear from the face of the earth. Maybe that's the answer.

I write to tell myself that I am getting better. I'm not going to give up. She wouldn't want me to. I should get back in the swing of things.

The swing of things?

The Room of Loneliness

You spend too much time in here, she whispered.

You built the room, didn't you? Carved these rooms in my heart. So here I am!

The old man was angry. Angry at her. Why did she leave?

She waited, then said, Kismet. We were destined.

He softened his voice. Yes. Destiny. That explains everything, or nothing. I don't know anymore.

Tell me.

Life. What is it? Why am I here, and you there? With you my life had meaning. Now? Nada.

She drew near. From across the great distance that separated them, her breath touched his face. He breathed in the fragrance of that unique perfume that was exquisitely her. Blindfolded, in a room with a thousand women, he could find her. He'd had a sense of her aroma from the time they met.

You're here?

Yes.

I must be dreaming.

"La vida es un sueño," the poet wrote. Life is a dream, an illusion. You used to say that.

La vida es un sueño, y los sueños sueño son.

I feel that truth more and more, he said. That's why we grow old, to understand the world is illusion. Curtains behind curtains, a continual stripping away of the veils that blind the soul. I feel I've become a character in a novel. But I'm not heroic. Just clinging on.

You're my hero, she said. At some point we have to leave things behind. Don't be afraid.

I'm not. Not anymore. Maybe when we were young and believed in the reality of things. Family, building a home, job, nice car, security . . . those deceiving phases of life.

Not deceiving, she whispered. Just phases. Perhaps we are caught in karma. Doing, then reaping. With time we begin to understand the illusions. Sometimes too late we seek the essence behind the colors that blind. As powerful as sunlight is, it does not reveal the essence. It creates colors, and we call those colors reality. Take away light and all disappears.

Her thoughts teased him. As always.

He smiled. Remember the story? If the universe goes completely pitch-black and all colors disappear, will we still bump into the kitchen table? Or will the table disappear?

Would we bump into God in the dark?

He chuckled. Bumping into God. What a beautiful image, if a bit scary. If you believe, he said.

We keep wondering, she replied.

They had searched for beauty and truth in their lives. Where was God? Was God the universe?

God is pure spirit. He is the light.

Pure spirit has no sex, she said.

But we keep on saying he.

We're trapped in a male-oriented language. Once men gained control of language they killed the goddess.

It's been tragic for women since goddesses were eclipsed from history. Men write history for and about themselves.

Catholics have Mary, he said.

True. The male hierarchy had to accept her because the people demanded her. We need the mother, and goddesses are mothers. They gave rise to great religions and beautiful stories.

And man killed the myths of the goddess.

Maybe our daughters will return to honor the goddess.

We can only hope.

If God is the Light and the Way, all is spirit. Can the material world be wedded to spirit? Opposites. I am still in the flesh, you in spirit. Can we remain in our mystical marriage?

She sighed. I don't know. But I have a curious feeling— she hesitated.

He waited.

. . . that somehow I might inherit form again. Inherit the earth.

I think of you coming in the form of a dove. Each day you come to the garden. Does soul move into a new body? He sat up straight, his curiosity piqued.

You see me as a dove. You desire to see me again. Is our love of the earth so strong we struggle against obscurity? We do not want to die.

Fear death?

Yes.

Follow your fear.

Yes.

The dove is how I see you. Is it my need to have you in a new reincarnation? Do I believe?

She waited, then leaned close, whispering, You said you had learned to leave things behind.

"Not you!" he cried out. "Never!"

Is that why you sit in the Room of Loneliness?

"Yes," he murmured.

Did he want her so badly that he had created a way of seeing her? Did others who lost their loved ones do this? Everyone wanting the departed back. Was it natural?

He felt empty. Even happy memories seemed to cause sorrow. Had he grown selfish in his mourning? Was he wanting her so much that he was making up stories, making believe she came in the form of a dove? Did he really believe in reincarnation?

I try to understand, to make sense of your leaving—

A mystery, she said, and yet it's as natural as the life of our species on earth. I'm thankful we had our time together.

Me too, he said. Death is constant. But somehow it was always out there, or it happened to others, or in books and movies . . .

"I didn't want us to end!" he shouted.

The dogs came running. What's up? How can we help? they seemed to say. Their master was the center of their world, and they sensed his pain.

"Nothing, nothing," he said, petting them. Faithful companions, always at his side. "It's okay, it's okay," he assured them. "Sorry I shouted." He cocked an ear and turned to listen.

Tell me, he said.

So much of our understanding comes from our bodies, she whispered. Our senses bring us great joy, yet they also deceive us. If karma means anything, it means being imprisoned in the self. We begin to think self will never die.

Introspection, he said. Spirit caught in the flesh, wishing it could live forever.

Resurrection, she said. Death and resurrection, the oldest theme on earth. The god dies, is buried, and from his flesh is born a corn plant, or a flower, or a coconut tree. Christ's blood and flesh in the Eucharist and wine. We eat and partake in the myth.

Do I need to be reborn? the old man asked.

Don't stay locked in this room. Come into the garden.

Her concern pushed him to get up. He rubbed his eyes, picked up his cane, and walked outside. The dogs followed him, eager to explore.

The dove alighted on the fence, its sad cry calling its mate.

"You," he whispered. It was the form he wished her spirit had taken. But he didn't believe. Could one live without form? Could one live as pure spirit?

The ancients had written about memory, a powerful force in the life of man. Now the muse of memory was haunting him.

He loved poetic metaphors, but he knew he couldn't give form to spirit. Only God could do that, he thought. He couldn't say the magic word and have her appear. He would never again hold her in his arms.

Where was she?

On a journey in the world of spirits, meeting her parents, grand-parents, old friends—

"They will take care of you," he said, his voice ripping the fabric of silence in the garden. His voice dark green in the encroaching evening.

Her journey into the world of spirits was a new adventure, but damn! He knew nothing of that world! He could only imagine it! Like imagining heaven. He worried. Was she okay? What if she lost the way? But she loved adventure. It was part of her nature. Now she had entered a country of spirits, from which no one returned.

Her spirit had lingered a while. Shortly after she died he had seen her walking down the hollyhock path. Dressed in a flowing Mexican skirt, the bright colors she loved, and a white blouse, stepping as lightly as an angel. She had turned and looked at him.

I'm going, she had said.

She disappeared down the path into the spring-blue of sky and rising clouds. Right at the spot where he was now standing.

Taking a Shower

He came in sweating. The summer heat was hitting ninety. In the mornings he worked in the garden. The tomato vines were beginning to produce, the lawn had to be mowed, flower beds needed to be raked and watered. He loved the smell of freshly turned earth, the green of crushed leaves. My mother's people were farmers, he had often told her. That was long ago in the Valley of the Moon.

She, too, came from farming stock, and she vividly remembered fond visits to her grandparents' Indiana farm. Later her parents had moved to the flat wheat fields of west Kansas, where she spent her childhood. As a grown woman she never looked back.

"Nothing for me there," she once said. "I'm New Mexican now."

"Chicana," he said, proud that she had stood by him in the work they were setting in motion. The Mexican American community was taking up arms against a sea of neglect, students marched for equal rights, César Chávez marched for campesinos.

Dirt and grass clippings were clinging to him, making him itch. But he felt good. The earth and its produce were real. The blazing sun was real. Water running down the vegetable rows was real.

A time when he engaged reality fully.

He read old myths, stories about gods and their relationships to tribes of the earth. Still happening, he thought. Look. The spirit of God shone in the shimmering leaves. Quetzalcóatl blooming. Buddha sitting on a tomato vine, a flower emerging from his belly button.

He decided he would sit in the kitchen while he drank a cold beer, then take a shower.

He hurried in but paused at the door. Taken by her beauty. She stood at the stove cooking fresh corn with squash simmering in cream. Roasted green chile to spice the pinto beans. His favorite meal, the rich kitchen fragrances of home.

"You look lovely," he said.

So it had been— patterns. He took care of some things, she others. Over the years their lives had established patterns.

She had learned to cook nuevo mexicano food, absorbing the New Mexican soul, its food, cultures, Spanish. She knew the history of the state and the Chicano struggle for social justice and better educational opportunities. Over the years they had invited many writers and artists to their home. She welcomed them, listened to them, joined La Causa.

She supported the African American civil rights movement and women's battle for equality; she riled against hierarchies that kept women oppressed. She fought for women's rights, for equal rights for every person. She questioned economic and political powers that kept people from living to their full potential.

More than his wife, she was his soul mate. Their ways converged. Maybe the beginning had its rough spots. Who the hell doesn't have to adjust to marriage, he thought. He was no saint. She was full of grace. Love prevailed.

Both taught school, so summers were for traveling. They visited Spain and brought home images that lasted a lifetime. The sun setting on Toledo, Museo del Prado, the Parador in León, the Barcelona of Gaudí. They studied the Spanish Civil War and enjoyed conversations with a friend in Cuernavaca who had fought in the Abraham Lincoln Brigade. Picasso's *Guernica* . . .

Almost time to eat, she said, smiling. Simple things like him taking care of the garden were rewarded with her smile, and always she thanked him. "You take such good care of our home."

He ran upstairs, jumped in the shower, and washed away the sweat, splashing and scrubbing with sudsy soap. A sensual reward. He towel-dried vigorously, fully aware of the body's pleasant sensations. He put on clean clothes and hurried down to the kitchen.

She was the real worker bee. What did he do? Write stories.

His stomach growled. Already he could taste the meal. Rich aromas filled the kitchen.

"Shall I turn on the air conditioner?" he asked.

"Not yet," she replied. The kitchen was warm, but she liked it that way. Warmth was essential to her. She would sit all day on the Mazatlán beach if he didn't insist on a time limit. Too much sun was not good for her fair skin.

She moved around the kitchen with ease. As a young woman she had taught dance and hadn't lost the rhythm, the graceful way of carrying herself.

He was thankful for many things, especially for her love. Full of grace meant full of love.

I'm a lucky man, he thought. Something stirred in him. Love was more than sensual need— it was part of the beauty she created in their lives.

"How about a little?" he asked from the table, where he sat drinking his beer.

"I'm cooking," she replied.

"You look done to me," he teased.

She laughed. Her laughter added to his need.

"I mean after lunch."

"We'll see," she said, teasing back.

What a satisfying life, he thought. He could already feel her under him in the summer heat, hear the slapping sound two moist bodies make. He guessed summer was their favorite time for making love.

Every season has its rewards. Love for all seasons. He thought it would never end.

"I'm a lucky man," he said to her.

She turned toward him from where she stood at the stove. "What a lovely thing to say."

"Does that mean . . .

"We'll see," she answered.

He finished his beer. "I love you," he said, seeking to describe his appreciation in words.

She put aside the skillet and went to him.

As graceful as a gazelle, he thought. His heart pounded, blood coursed through his body.

She kissed his forehead, kissed his salty lips. Her tongue was sweet, warm.

"You taste of sweat," she said, gazing into his eyes. Her eyes expressed her love. When she looked at him her eyes spoke love. Understanding. Affection. Everything.

He was hungry. For everything.

The old man started up the stairs, holding on to the handrail, remembering to go slow. One step at a time. His lower back hurt. One leg dragged. Sciatica. Pinched nerve. Arthritis. All from a spinal cord injury when he was a kid. Now age had brought back the weakness, pain in the old, fractured bones.

He sat on the toilet seat, slowly taking off his shirt, pants, and shoes, thinking, Here is where she fell. He could still hear her calling him. Cries that rocked his emotions.

Sometimes at night he thought he heard her call. He couldn't sleep.

Old people know bathrooms are dangerous places.

He placed a rubber mat on the shower floor and turned on the water. He reached for the grab bar, closed the door, and reached for a wash cloth and soap. Everything took time, especially reaching down and scrubbing his feet. His back hurt. Need a stool in here, he thought. Hard to bend down.

Even taking a shower had become a chore. Took forever. When he was done he sat on the toilet seat and towel-dried himself. He wouldn't shave. What for?

He looked in the mirror and laughed. "I got old," he said.

He dressed slowly. I'm running out of clean underwear. Need a new pair of shoes, but don't like going out. I haven't bought clothes since she left. Don't like crowds at the mall. Best to stay home, here in the silence.

I say I don't have time, he thought, and time's all I've got.

How strange time had become. It changed all right. As they got older time had sped up. Einstein said if a person rode a speeding spaceship he would get younger. The clock turned back. Not true—getting old meant time went faster.

They had retired, so there should have been more time to read, go to movies, see friends, rest. No, time flowed faster than a rushing river. Was it just a feeling? Mortality calling?

"It's not gravity that bends time, it's old age." Muttering, he walked down the stairs, one at a time, holding the railing.

The kitchen was empty, silent.

What will I eat today? Maybe warm some soup. Drive over to the barrio and have some enchiladas? Nah. Don't like to sit alone in a restaurant. Not for me!

He had seen old men eating alone. He felt sorry for them.

He didn't want to bother family either. And the old gals at the senior center had their own problems. One had just had all her teeth pulled. No sense inviting her to lunch. They all suffered. Getting fat. Colitis. Bloated stomachs. Knee bone grating against knee bone. Cancer, heart problems . . . on and on.

Some had lost their entire life savings in the bad economy. Brokers had promised a killing in hedge funds that didn't deliver. The seniors played bingo and lamented. "Nothing left," they whispered. "Maybe find a man," one woman said. Two Social Security checks were better than one. Just barely making it.

Warm up some soup, the old man thought. A salad would be nice. The doctor on TV said to eat a salad every day.

Quiet as a tomb.

He guessed it was the silence in the house that created the sadness in his heart.

Silence was a killer.

He remembered a song. The sound of silence. Like a bridge over troubled waters, I will lay me down. What did they know! No one knows silence like a lonely old man.

Anyway, he wasn't hungry anymore. He went to the buffet, picked up her photograph, and spoke to her, loving words, telling her how much he missed her. Clutching the photograph to his chest, he lay down on the floor. Curled up like a baby. He thought his heart would break with sadness.

I Must Be Going Crazy

The old man awoke with a headache. He hadn't eaten. Anyway, eating wasn't a priority. Thousands of meals eaten together, and now the table was empty. Outside the setting sun cast a golden light on the garden, hummingbirds skimmed the hollyhocks, a robin unearthed dry leaves.

The red-breasted bird was a daily visitor, hopping about, pausing, head cocked to the ground . . . listening.

The Word of God was stuck in the earth.

"Bendito sea Dios."

The old man said a blessing every morning, as was his custom.

"Grandfather Sun, bless all of life."

He asked the saints to bless and keep his wife, his parents, brothers and sisters, friends— all in the spirit world now. Too many gone. He prayed for the hungry and suffering children of Africa.

"I should've been a rabbi," he told himself.

He made coffee, fed the dogs, then walked outside and looked at the garden. The robin had flown, marking a season.

The dove had not yet arrived. He loved to see the dove come to sit on the fence, then alight to drink at the water bowl. Graceful in flight.

He watched birds, those in the neighborhood that were regulars, each kind arriving in its own time. Cranes and geese followed the river's course, south in fall, north in spring. In the North Valley farmers planted fields of grain for wintering geese, and down near Socorro was the Bosque del Apache, a large bird reserve.

The ancients had watched the flight of birds, how and where they flew. Such movements foretold the fortunes of kings. Hadn't Caesar been warned?

"I love birds," the old man whispered. Birds evolved from dinosaurs, a beautiful mystery he could trust. Evolution, handiwork of the Great Mystery.

He wanted to believe the dove held her spirit, her soul returned. Reincarnation? Anything to hold on to.

Two doves flew in and perched on the fence.

"Ah, you have a friend!" he said and laughed. "Good!"

He didn't want her to be alone in the world of spirits. He thought he knew the world of departed souls, but he really didn't. He had described the afterlife in the stories he wrote, but real knowledge of the place? No one knew, no one had ever returned.

Where was she? He worried.

The Word of God was absent from the earth. Or was it just his heart that was empty?

An extreme drought had come over the land, like droughts described in the Bible. Locusts swarmed, eating the flesh of anything green, bark beetles destroying piñon trees. Forest fires spread throughout the West.

He wanted to believe the Word of God would bless the earth. He needed something to hold on to, but the eastern slope of the Jemez Mountains was going up in flames.

Everything seemed futile. Empty.

Get a life! Get up and get out!

Brush your teeth, comb your hair, do something. Grief is killing you. Enough sorrow, enough of what happened last night. Sleeping on the floor won't bring her back. All the tears on earth won't bring her back! Don't be a victim! She wants you to get on with your life!

He looked at her photograph. Her face lit up, she smiled. Yes, you have to move on.

He knew, but he had no enthusiasm for getting out. No energy. Death, the most natural of life's consequences, had come to rob him of his Beloved. Her body had collapsed, like the universe eventually collapsing back into its original cell. A singularity, the scientists called it.

Her soul had joined a multitude of angels, spirits in that world unknown to common man.

Once, the universe had expanded from a pinpoint of light, God's original energy, still growing, still expanding. Was there spirit involved in the damned thing? Of course there was. The whole enchilada was animated with spirit, from the sea slug to the soaring eagle. A universal consciousness was born when the Big Bang exploded. He believed. Then the nagging question: Was there a God consciousness before the Big Bang? A Buddha thought waiting to happen?

Earthlings evolved from a cell of light, and billions of light years later would return to one cell. In the meantime, the human task was to keep Mother Earth safe from harm. The earth was awake, alive, aware. Be part of her awareness— find the rhythm and dance to it.

"That's our work," the old man said. He praised the young who worked at saving the environment. Saving earth.

The original fish-like ancestors had probably crawled out of an ancient sea to escape predators. From the very beginning, the big fish ate the little fish. Nothing had changed. Mankind would eventually destroy itself. Nuclear war, the new singularity. The world has become one big, people-eating corporation.

Her passage had not happened all at once. She had slowly grown weaker. Together they had sought out doctors, then the pain medications began to take their toll. But throughout the long winter an aura of serenity had lit up her face, peace resided in her fragile hands, love sounded sweetly in her final whispers.

She went gentle into the night eternal.

Still, he couldn't accept the finality of her death. He resisted. Some called it denial. He had stayed at her side, been as attentive as he could, caring for her, feeding her, sleeping in the chair beside her hospice bed, a witness to a passage neither of them had ever imagined. It was the beginning of a new journey.

———

"How do you feel?" he asked her.

"Going south," she replied, smiling.

The four sacred directions were intrinsic to the worldview of many Native American communities. The emblem on the New Mexico state flag was the Zia symbol, a bright sun with lines radiating out in the four directions. South was the source of life. She was returning to the life source. The old man understood her words. Her cosmology was complete, harmonious, a sign of her inner wisdom.

Yes, going south.

Her end loosened a lifetime of emotions in him. Simple things they had shared those final months brought tears to his eyes.

He had thought he knew about death. He had read myths and holy books that described the afterlife for many cultures. Heaven and hell, Valhalla, Hades, the Buddha's path, nirvana, Mictlan of the Aztecs, the Tibetan bardo where souls circulated before reincarnating— something like the Catholic's Purgatory? A world of spirits.

When the old man was young he had taken up the pen and discovered the world of spirits. At first he thought the characters and content for the stories he wrote were inspired by the people he knew. He was grounded in his native place, New Mexico and its history. He believed in reality.

And it's true, that was his background, but the more he wrote the more he felt the pull of the spirit world. The voice of the story was not completely his. He was moved to write the tragedies and comedies of those characters who came to visit him.

Write my story, each said. Commandments from the spirit world.

His first novel was inspired by the spirit of an old curandera, a healer who assisted the people of the eastern plains country.

He told his students that in the process of writing he had become a shaman. Characters who wanted their story told came to him in visions. His imagination was his soul, and that meant his soul could fly to the world of spirits.

What do you mean? his students asked. Do characters actually appear? They tell you to write their stories?

There is no actuality... a vision is a vision. He tried to explain. The story becomes actual, some form of reality on paper or in your computer. Digital reality. There, is that actual enough for you!

The spirit world resides in my creative imagination, he wrote. A world beyond will, reason, and action, a universe beyond ordinary reality. But the spirits have so much energy they seem to fly beyond the cage of my soul. Do they create heaven? Or do we?

He had learned that reason and will could not transport him to the world of spirits. His imagination was the chariot he rode to a world of dream images, legendary creatures, exotic and often fearful stories, mythological characters, the commandments of foreign gods, dark stuff— and glory be! Light! The revelations of his imagination also brought enlightening illuminations.

The writer was the hero who went deep into the imagination and returned, holding in hand a gritty story he could write and share with the world. If the story got published the writer could say to his readers, there, that's proof of my journey.

God planted the seed, humans evolved, the seed in the primal brain grew. It was still there. Dreams and creativity could reveal the mind's contents.

Our inheritance, the old man thought.

A shaman knew a person fell ill when trauma shattered the soul. The shaman flew in search of the fractured soul and put the pieces together. Reintegration. A healing process.

The soul was the creative imagination, its creativity knew no boundaries. The spirit world resided in the individual soul and spiraled into the Universal Soul.

His thoughts were taking him deeper and deeper into new realizations. He wondered where the search for his wife would take him.

The real question: Where is she?

Had she gone to meet Randy Lopez, one of his recent characters?

Did the characters of all the stories ever written reside with the souls of the departed? When one died, might one by chance meet the prophet Isaiah conversing with Don Quixote?

If all the good, departed souls were there, might demons also appear?

He couldn't explain it. Like trying to explain her photograph on the buffet. She was in the photograph, her soul animated the picture. But try as he might, he could not bring her back.

What good was being a shaman if he couldn't contact his Beloved? He knew many tried to contact the departed. Most did it for love, for example a wife wanting to know how her husband was doing. Or where he left the insurance policy.

Mediums of every sort appeared, claimed they could channel the departed.

"Quackery!" the old man said. Not for me. I'll do it my way!

She was the essence of his soul, but death had cut the tether of love and unity. The gold cord that once connected him to her was severed.

He was drinking and singing, "Good night, Irene . . . Irene, good night. Good night, Irene, good night, Irene . . . I'll see you in my dreams . . ."

A sad song from long ago.

He felt he was going crazy. Was grief carrying him toward an endgame, a tragedy?

The dark voices of depression whispered, Why go on?

Don't listen! she answered. You wrote that the curandera would come in your hour of need! Listen! Go out! Fear not! Find someone to care for!

"Ah, damn!" he cursed. "It's not that easy."

She knew. She wept for him, and he felt her sadness.

The photograph shed tears. "Bendito sea Dios," he whispered and kissed her face. Blessed be God.

Was he going crazy? Or was there hope?

They had discussed death, and during those last months he

thought they had understood its meaning— a fading of the flesh, but the essence would move on. A new adventure waited.

The world of spirits was as complex as the world they called real. Two worlds separated only by a thin veil. When he was deep in the writing of a story, the veil parted and he entered the world of spirits. Then his characters came alive, talked, argued, filled his writing room with their presence.

He wrote every day, and when he had finished the morning's work, she always asked him how it went. Every day, day in and day out, recorded in the syllables of his stories, she knew he cast aside the veil of separation.

In her quest she, too, had crossed into the world of ideas. She ingested everything she read, and she shared her adventures with him. Books filled her with joy. Her eyes lit up as she told him of newfound knowledge that came to fulfill her. She, too, knew how to fly.

She spread the tarot cards on the table.

See . . .

Yes.

She knew. She had searched deep and wide.

It was like making love. The flesh giving up its ecstasy, becoming spirit, becoming god. Eternal love. Love was the bond that united them, the glowing aura that surrounded them.

They could fly. They shared their adventures in the confines of their home. Home was safety. It centered them. They could fill their souls to the brim, journey into the knowledge books held, and return.

That's why writers cannot give up their secrets, he thought. As Emily Dickinson once cautioned, don't tell or they'll come and take us away. Those who have never torn aside veils of illusion and flown to other worlds wouldn't understand. They were stuck in reality.

But death? When it finally came, he felt lost.

Easy enough for others to understand. She's gone to heaven they said. She's at rest. She's with the angels—

Not so fast! the old man protested. If it were that easy I wouldn't feel like I'm going crazy! Her soul was torn from mine. I lost my anchor.

So don't give me easy answers! I'll find her on my own!

Heaven or hell. Where? In the mind. And why resurrection? Had her spirit been reborn in a new body? Is that what it meant?

We all fear death. A history of fear. Follow your fear to the very end and wish for immortality. That's why the priests of the early tribes proposed an afterlife. Something had to be left after the body quit and was laid in the earth.

They had read Egyptian mythology together, visited the Valley of the Kings. Resurrection was as old as humankind.

For him the answer had to be in the world of spirits. But he was beginning to doubt.

He was wrestling with the most profound conflict in his life.

Where? Why?

The entire world is animated by spirit. The universal consciousness, I feel it. She bathed in sunlight, she watched the moon. She felt connected to the stars.

Daily he prayed to the ancestors to take care of her soul. She was out there. Nightly and at sunrise he gave thanks and asked those who had gone before to bless her. The ancestors were constant. They were embedded in memory.

He talked to her at the most curious moments. A stranger passing by might think he was crazy. That's what crazy people did, wasn't it? Talk to themselves.

Downtown, the homeless hung out around the bus depot, the alleys, the rescue mission where lunch was served. Those possessed talked to themselves, walked the streets mumbling, carrying their worldly possessions in backpacks or grocery carts.

He didn't want to end up like that.

"Enough!" he said.

Yes! she answered.

Downtown

The old man decided to drive downtown. He hadn't been there in ages. In the past, when they had lunch downtown, she always suggested they drive home via Central, the main street that was once upon a time Route 66. Okie Ave. Memories of the Dust Bowl and the Great Depression.

Lowriding? he joked.

Yes, she said. Our town.

A lot of history written in asphalt. If only the streets and the old buildings could talk.

That's what writers are for, she nudged him and smiled.

They were a couple of happy old-timers cruising the main drag. They loved the place. He pointed at the high school he had attended.

The school had recently been converted into apartments. Yuppie lofts, he called them. Downtown had grown, and yet in many ways, it remained the same. Funky.

You like funky.

Sure, honey. The city still has character. Antiseptic doesn't appeal to me.

They loved the rough and tumble of the cultural groups. Gringo yuppies, politicians climbing the ladder to the numero uno rung, attorneys of every stripe, Chicanos joining the bandwagon while trying to stay true to their heritage, Hispanics who could no longer speak Spanish, the Pueblo people caught between their traditions and modernity, all required to speak the common tongue: English.

And us trying to hold on to our mother tongue, the old man said. How can we pray to our ancestors if we forget the language they taught us?

She reached across and touched him, a comforting gesture.

He smiled. Always felt better when she touched him.

Workers from Mexico were doing heavy labor. Good, he thought. Let them come. Asian communities were developing— their restaurants told part of their story. The city's growing pains, the country's northern cultures moving into the southwest. Inevitable.

Change, she said. She believed in change. Let them come.

And always the homeless, the dispossessed, the poor, and 'Nam veterans on the streets.

Have things have gotten better?

Yes, slowly, she assured him.

The old YMCA building stood on that corner, he pointed and continued his litany of remembrances. Times past.

We went swimming there. They tore the place down. The Sunshine Theatre. Saturday movies at the Kimo. Remember?

Yes, she said. She forgot nothing. Forgetting came later.

Payless Drugs on the corner. Now gone. All the old landmarks, gone.

We're here, she said. She had no fear.

She always lived in the present, but she relished the stories he told about the downtown he had known as a young man. His stories made the place come alive— 1950s alive. She could see him walking down the street with his friends, strutting in jeans and T-shirts, rock 'n' roll pachucos swinging to Fats Domino and Bill Haley, playfully eyeing the high school girls.

She turned to him. You were cool.

Sure, hijita. Puro daddy-o!

They laughed.

And girls?

I had to turn them away.

You've kept your good looks.

Gracias. You're the loveliest woman in 'Burque. In the whole wide world.

Oh, sí.

He reached for her hand. Such had been moments of their love as they drove up to their home on the west side.

Now the old man drove the streets alone, looking for a parking place. Everything had changed. New restaurants, bars, City Hall Mall where stood Rivera's sculpture of a prior mayor.

He was remembering some of the old-timers who had built the city. Now footnotes in history books. Nothing lasts. Todo se acaba, my dad used to say. Everything ends.

And love? she asked.

Love is forever. I will always love you.

I know, she said. Lovers forever.

I wrote that on many a Valentine's Day card.

Yes.

She kept his love poems. She read hundreds of books and made notes. Passages that revealed truths. Lists of words to look up. Meanings. Esoteric gospels of life. The pulsing of the universe. Mother Nature's revolt against the killing toxins mankind was laying on her breast. Mayan and Essene prophecies. The downfall of the goddess, the hierarchy of man.

She read tarot cards, but never divulged the Death card.

It will all fall down, she said. Prophetic.

An active mind full of revelations. A soul of wisdom.

"You were my Sophia," the old man whispered.

Leaning onto his cane, he walked stiffly into the mall and found a bench. He felt out of place. Around him the excessive rush and noise of people he no longer recognized. City workers, spiders caught in the web of time, money, and politics.

He was sweating by the time he sat down. Not my heart, he thought. Doc checked it. Just the people. Not used to the madding crowd. Maybe I shouldn't have come.

The mall was a gathering place for the homeless hanging out till lunch was served at the Baptist mission and 'Nam veterans still hurting from the shock and poisons of war. Now they were joined by those who had fought in the sands of the Fertile Crescent. War games for every generation, crippling.

The homeless women looked tired, forlorn. Toting their backpacks, they followed their men as the Adelitas of the Mexican Revolution had once followed their warriors.

"La cucaracha, la cucaracha, ya no puede caminar . . ."

But these women didn't struggle for social justice or land reform, just keeping alive day to day was goal enough. They were subject to abuse, rape, hunger, addictions, sleepless nights under overpass bridges, cardboard camps in the river forest, freezing on winter nights. They stood on street corners with signs that read Out of Luck, Need Money For Gas, Hungry, Can You Help Me Get a Meal?

Was it luck? Fate or destiny? Why so much trauma in life? The old man grew pensive.

Once, he had enjoyed people-watching. He looked at shoes. He could tell a lot from the shoes people wore. On the street, at lectures, on the beach, summer or winter shoes, or dressy high heels for restaurant dining, shoes told a story. He remembered his mother stuffing in pieces of cardboard to cover the holes in his worn-out school shoes. Good for one more day.

Even at church he found himself looking at shoes, those of the repentant and the not-so-repentant. Women's shoes sometimes aroused the erotic, why deny it? Summer sandals and painted toenails were killers.

Ah, those were the days.

People were the content of his stories, his stock-in-trade, his livelihood. Writers write about people and nature, but Mother Nature was losing the battle, the environment was going to hell.

Why so much autism and allergies? And in the human-created preservative-filled and sugar-coated environment, obesity. Drugs killing the young.

Now the hurrying crowd made him dizzy. Late and soon, everything was spent. We lay waste our power.

He needed water. His mouth was dry.

Concentrate, he told himself. Pick individuals. It's the lone wolf who writes the story, not the pack. But the pack makes the wolf, alpha males and females.

You are my alpha female, he whispered, feeling her presence.

Of course, she answered. You wouldn't have it any other way.

Her response made him feel better. Yes, a lovely alpha female came to fill my life. I loved every minute.

He studied people. The way they walked, talked, what they wore, how the business types greeted each other. The homeless, scraggly as they were, got close when they hugged. Business men shook hands, but kept each other at a distance.

In Mexico City men greeted each other with an abrazo. Were Latin men more at ease? Or was it a cultural thing, something that came from the time men hugged to check if the other guy was carrying a pistol?

All this was story stuff, but now he felt the juices go dry. The women interested him for a while. Skirt lengths had gone up. Lovely creatures. He thought about sex. Long ago.

Then his heart stopped. The woman passing in front of him startled him. He struggled to get up, pushing on his cane. He called, "Hijita!"

The woman in a bright-patterned blouse and colorful Mexican skirt didn't turn.

"It's her!" he cried. "My Beloved! From where?"

She pushed a grocery cart full of clothes. His throat went dry; he couldn't form the vowels of her name.

"Amor!" he called. "Wait!"

She had returned! He knew she would! He hurried after her, stumbling.

She stopped and greeted two homeless men.

His heart was racing. It's her! My Beloved! A miracle!

She knew the men. One lit a cigarette for her, the other looked around and surreptitiously handed her a sack-enclosed bottle.

"Amor! Querida!" The old man struggled toward her, his voice hoarse, choking . . . he was falling.

What the hell is going on? How? She's here! I recognize her blouse and skirt! Her walk! It's her!

His heart was pounding. A couple of kids on skateboards came swooshing by and almost toppled him. He nearly did fall. A man caught him.

"Be careful, old man."

A helpful warning, or impertinence. The old just got in the way. Worse than the homeless. Why didn't they just stay home? The mall was no place for them. A nuisance.

The old man dragged forward, holding himself up with the cane, feeling a heart attack coming on.

He called again. "Wait! Wait!"

He heard her laughter. She drank from the bottle and turned to face him. He stopped short. She looked at him with cold, gray eyes. A face lined with years of hard life.

It wasn't her! But the blouse! The skirt! They're hers! I'd recognize them anywhere!

The woman said something to the two men. They glanced at the old man, then turned and walked away.

His heart fell, sinking to the pit of his stomach. He groaned. A painful cry tore at his throat, but stuck there. His knees gave way, he was falling.

A man rushed forward and took his arm.

"You okay?" He helped him to a bench.

"Is he drunk?" a woman asked.

"Should we call the paramedics?"

"Needs to sit . . ."

"Looks okay. You okay?"

He sat. The voices faded, the shadows moved away.

Then he remembered.

He had donated her clothes to a shelter for homeless women. The blouse and skirt the woman was wearing truly had once graced his wife's body.

He had given it all away, emptied the closets. A ritual played out by those who lose a loved one.

Empty closets, a metaphor.

The Saints

He sat, out of breath, trembling . . .

Those who had helped him to the bench had moved on, the busy people of the city.

The old man had followed Jesus into the shadows, and now he wondered if he were alive or dead.

The homeless moved on. Always.

Everyone was moving on. Spirits. All moving in slow motion.

I should have known, he thought.

Time to move on. I'm seeing things, seeing her in that woman. Ridiculous! I am become ridiculous. Is that how he wanted to end his life? A ridiculous old man.

Constipated half the time. Having to get up at night to pee. Prostate enlarged. Arthritis. Joints hurt. Hard to bend over. Couldn't make it with the old gals at the senior center— didn't want to. Not anymore. Had other things on his mind.

What things? Food molding in the refrigerator, not seeing friends, eating only raisin bran and bananas, milk going sour. Less and less interest in people. He didn't garden anymore— his nephew took care of the yard and maintenance, his niece brought food. Caretakers.

He appreciated them, but he didn't want to be a liability. Old people can do less and less. I have a young mind in an old body, he cursed. Reality encroaching.

"I have my Beloved," he whispered. In the photograph. He had convinced himself her soul was in the picture.

He needed her to be *in* the photograph, otherwise he didn't know where she was. Her essence had moved into the world of spirits, and that world wasn't a cute place with safe boundaries. Not like heaven.

Oh no, she was on a new journey, new adventures, no maps, no signposts, everybody moving on, and if she was lucky she might meet family members and old friends. They could travel together. Never mind the moaning wind blowing around the edges of the spirit world, she could find a safe harbor, perhaps a new home.

There was a place beyond— that's what he had written in the Randy Lopez story. She loved the story, fell in love with the character, said maybe she would meet him there on the other side. En el otro barrio, the mexicanos said. The neighborhood beyond this one.

Yeah, there could exist purpose . . . on the other side. But the spirit world wasn't a place, it was something nebulous he couldn't put his finger on. Damn! Truth was he didn't know what the world of spirits looked like! Any more than anyone knew the outline of heaven! It was all imagination! Stories told by numerous tribes over the millennia!

He was raised a Catholic. His mother had taught him to pray to plaster statues of saints she kept on her altar. Rosaries to the Virgin Mary. As a child he believed the Virgin's soul was embedded in the statue. She heard his prayers. Otherwise, why pray?

The statue or picture of any saint was animated by the soul of the saint. Ancient animism.

The photograph held his wife's soul, her essence.

It had to be!

Yes, that's the way it was.

New Mexican santeros painted retablos, images of saints on wood panels. Sacred wood cut from the trees of life— cottonwood roots from the river valley, piñon trees from the hills. Trees were essential. Every tree represented the greater Tree of Life.

The faithful bought retablos and had them blessed by their parish priest. The faithful prayed to images of the saints. Faith was a river flowing through New Mexico, the essence of thanks for all that was.

Had the old man lost his faith?

He remembered a story. An old woman, a believer, spoke to her favorite saint, Saint Lucia. She prayed to the small statue: Santa Lucia, if you restore my eyesight, I will pray a rosary to you every night. But if you don't answer my prayer then I'll put you in the closet.

When the woman died her children found Saint Lucia's statue in a closet along with the statues of several other saints who had not answered their mother's prayers. Qué lástima.

The old man laughed.

Any saint could be cajoled. Saint Christopher, I had your medal swinging on my car's rear view mirror, but I still got in a wreck. I don't care if I was drinking, you should have protected me! Into the glove compartment you go!

A never-ending conversation with the saints. With God. Dios mío, ayuda me. Did you hear me? I asked for help. Never mind, I'll do it myself!

In the most humble home, pictures of the Holy Family or the Heart of Jesus or the Virgin Mary hung on the walls. Or FDR's photograph. Some still kept Kennedy's photo. The people forgave his escapades. A man is just a man, they said.

A crucifix hung at every door. Mass on Sundays, holy days of obligation, the Stations of the Cross, evangelical sermons, Pueblo ceremonials, on and on the river of faith flowed as constant as the Rio Grande.

Why? the old man asked.

He had inherited his mother's crucifix. She had prayed to a doleful, pained Jesus on the cross. She believed the power of Jesus rested in the image. An archaic faith. Pagan worship, some would say. The priests from the East Coast had some difficulty understanding this kind of adoration. It was something in the Mexican way of life, and it dated back to the Old World. Back to when hunters painted animals on walls of caves. The primitive drawing held the animal's spirit; the hunter would prevail.

We kneel before the statue of the Virgin Mary and pour our hearts out, praying for intercession. She is alive in the statue. She looks down on us. She hears.

"My Beloved hears me," the old man said. But she doesn't answer. Is she lost in that vast world of spirits?

He still prayed to his mother's santos. La Virgen María, Jesucristo, San José, Santa Ana, Santo Niño de Atocha, San Martín. Plaster statues that once adorned her altar, bought long ago from a traveling salesman who swore they had been blessed by the pope.

His mother had them blessed by the local priest anyway. She knew better. Her santos would take care of her and her family. The Virgin Mary would watch over them.

He learned faith as a child. But what did he believe?

He had to renew his faith. How?

He looked around and felt his wife near him. Was she coming to him? Or was he going to her?

He had begun not to fear death. Felt curious at first, because it's bred in the flesh to fear the night eternal. That's why people go on living as long as they can. Fear of the night that never ends. Fear of being conscious in that sleep, perhaps to dream . . .

Follow your fear, some said, to the very depths of darkness. When you finally resolve your fear you will be liberated.

"Listen to me, old people," the old man said. "We don't have to be afraid."

Maybe he was no longer afraid because he felt her presence.

Hadn't he insinuated that he had become a shaman? A writer had to be a shaman. Stories were about lost souls. The characters came to him as spirits, and he gave them bone and flesh. In his visions, they asked to have their stories told.

He cursed. The two skateboarders who had nearly knocked him over were back. They stood looking at him.

"Talking to himself."

"Looney."

"Hey, old man, you crazy or what?"

A cop nearby called for the boys to clear out, and the two ran off.

"I'm no damn shaman," he said to himself. Just a tired old man believing she's near. But I can't reach her.

He thought he had the ability to communicate with the spirit world. Not just communicate, he could go there. He had entered that world many times, like Odysseus had entered Hades, like Jesus had walked in hell. Luke Skywalker and other mythic heroes from Hollywood movies had shaped new mythologies from the bare outlines of old myths.

Such heroes possessed shaman power, or so the legends told. The story made the man, the man became the story.

So it was with the characters who visited him, the spirits waiting to take on the flesh of the story.

That's how it was. Man becoming story. Stories in the wind. Like the gold leaves of October, millions. Only a few stories survived, but hidden in the core of every story lay the secret. Storytellers had visited the world of spirits. The writer's task was to enter that world and return.

His writings had taken him there. He was no mere trickster, no Coyote fabricating falsehoods, there was no Ariadne with cord to lead him out of the labyrinthine tales he composed. No! He was a true shaman!

He struggled to sit up.

"I'm no imposter!" he shouted.

Sit down, you'll fall. The presence bade him sit down.

You're here?

Yes.

I'm confused, he said. I thought you were gone.

You'll never lose me, she said. Don't you remember?

Lovers forever.

Yes. Forever.

I've been trying too hard. Thinking you're out there—

I'm here, she said.

But you became pure essence. I held you the night you took your last breath. Your soul left your body—

I didn't leave, she said. I'm here.

His heart grew calm, he felt comforted. You've been here all along?

Yes.

I should have known.

You did. But grief can cause confusion. You're alone and sad. Just know that I'm with you. In the photographs you keep in each room, in the flowers you bring me . . . I'm everywhere.

Yes. That's why I talk to you.

Of course.

So . . . I am a shaman.

You're the most handsome shaman in the world. But you're locked in your body. The flesh dreams . . . but after all, it is flesh. It confuses us with many paths to take. So many distractions.

She knew.

Even a shaman needs a guide?

Yes.

Thank you, he said and reached to kiss her hands. There's a veil keeping us apart.

It's an illusion, she replied. We are together. Our love allows us to be beyond space and time.

The old man smiled. Faith, he said.

Yes. You know what it's coming to.

Yes, but I'm afraid.

Don't be. I am here as long as you remember me.

That's it, he said. That's what he feared. She would be there *only* as long as he remembered her. Then what?

The future will take care of itself, she said. When it's time I'll come for you.

They went on talking. Yesterday, today, and into the night eternal. The veil was transparent, any shaman could see that. With love one could brush it aside.

The woman was wearing your clothes— ah, now he really remembered. Her daughters had emptied the closets. Coats, sweaters, dresses, skirts, so many bright patterns, dozens of shoes.

"She knew how to dress," the oldest had said.

"Yes."

They were extremely proud of their mother. Her intelligence, her sense of adventure, her wise counsel, the way she dressed and carried herself.

"She could make any skirt look sexy. She had the knack."

They had held up each piece of clothing. Remembering. They had kept a few, but most they stuffed into plastic bags. "For the women's shelter."

The old man had looked on. He knew every garment, the fragrance each held, special times worn. Like the boat cruise on the Nile, the way she had dressed for the dance. Silk dresses she bought at a market in Xian. Mexican skirts from the mercados. Macy's. Dillard's. Each garment held a memory.

"She loved shoes. She had lovely feet, and lovely legs to boot. Everything about her fit just right."

The old man nodded and grew sad at the memory. Why did such loveliness pass away? Why did she leave?

They continued emptying the closets. He had sat, observing, saying little. The daughters were grieving, each in her own way. They loved their mother, and she loved them. Deep. Parting with her clothes wasn't easy for them, but it needed to be done.

A sad ritual.

Later, he had taken the bags to the homeless shelter. They had given him a gift receipt for tax purposes. Part of the banalities of death, he was learning.

That is my wish, she had told him. Homeless women will wear my dresses, walk in my shoes. Let them walk the streets in bright patterns. All colors fade with time, but for the moment let my sisters walk proud!

Don Quixote

There was a silly old man who lived in the province of La Mancha in Spain. Few remember his real name, if he'd ever had a real name. His story is a fiction, as are all stories ever written. The author called his hero Don Quixote, Knight of the Sorrowful Face.

Something like that.

Don Quixote spent his dotage years reading the popular books of the time, novels that described the adventures of knights. The fantasies began to scramble his mind.

Don Quixote talked to himself, especially after he had spent days absorbed in one of his novels. I, too, can be a knight, he thought.

Plato outlawed poets from his republic— should we outlaw the reading of novels by old people? Fantasies are all the old have left. Fantasy upon fantasy.

The brain clogs up and the mind becomes a web of imaginations, story piled upon story, memory upon memory. Fanciful forgetting is nature's way.

The old man visited a nursing home during lunchtime. Men older than he were slurping down Jello. Just then a very attractive woman entered the dining hall. The old farts looked at her, but all they said was, "Hey, can I have more Jello?"

"Damn! They forget!" the old man said, and hurried out. No nursing home for me! I still have ganas! Urges in the blood.

But even those urges would slip away, he knew.

Let the old read novels. There may be some truths yet to be gleaned from those make-believe stories.

The old man spent most afternoons reading. His wife had been an avid reader. Nothing wrong with fantasizing, he thought.

Don Quixote put away the romance novels and decided to get real. He called his farmhand Sancho Panza. "My good man," he said, "it's not too late to serve justice, to save damsels in distress, and to dream the impossible dream."

This idea of the impossible dream became a theme in a popular musical centuries later. Thereafter, many a theater-goer believed the fantasy built upon a fantasy, they began to believe Don Quixote was real. Best to remember that plays, like novels, are fantasies. So are movies spun out by a mythology factory called Hollywood.

Why not indulge in fantasy? Don't our wise counselors tell us to follow our dreams? Follow our bliss. Sometimes the impossible dream is all that's left. Following the dream may be more hopeful than following one's fear. Or do they converge?

Like planets, do bliss and fear reach conjunction?

Sancho found and outfitted Quixote in an old, rusty suit of armor, of the sort now found only in museums.

Sancho the realist complained, "This is crazy!"

But Don Quixote talked Sancho into the adventure, promising him the governorship of an island. Sancho bought into the fantasy.

It's incredible how often people believe the dreamer, even if he or she is crazy. At times an entire country follows an insane leader. So it goes.

Don Quixote, astride his horse—Rocinante—and Sancho, on a burro, rode into the countryside, searching for evil-doers to befuddle.

Befuddle is as befuddle does.

The famous scene everyone remembers is Don Quixote charging the windmills. Sancho tried to warn him that a windmill is just a windmill, but Don Quixote didn't listen.

Deluded leaders don't listen to the common folk. Such are the tragedies of history.

Don Quixote spurred his horse forward, tilted at the windmill, and was quickly and resoundingly knocked on his ass.

Why the Don Quixote story?

Last night the old man had watched the movie on TV, and he had begun to think that every old man is a Don Quixote.

Half-crazy, still thinking there are just causes to be served. Dream the impossible dream, strike down windmills of poverty and racism, gather resources for shelters full of abused women, feed starving children—

What can an old man do?

In the end, Don Quixote is beaten by reality. He gives up his dream of being a knight. All his chivalry novels are burned.

Don't give up so easily, his wife whispered.

Dulcinea?

She laughed softly. I'm no Dulcinea, she said. Only the woman who loves you.

The old man smiled and stopped the soft rocking of his chair.

You are my Dulcinea. Ideal and real. The loveliest woman on earth. I thought I was forgetting you, but I still talk to you. I tell you everything.

I know, she said, sensing his sadness.

I thought with time the memories would slip away, one by one.

Your memories are windmills, she said. You've been tilting at memories.

"By God, you're right!" the old man said, standing and looking out at the garden, where the dove sat on the fence. "I'm struggling against memories. Why?"

The muse of memory brings joy, but she also brings pain. You know.

"Yes," the old man whispered. "I'm living too much with memories. Fantasizing. What's the answer?"

You need to create space for new memories. Go on a cruise or spend more time at our mountain cabin. More time with family, plant the rose bush you've been thinking about. Get in the car and drive around the city. Visit a friend. Learn to love again.

Love? I'm afraid, the old man protested. I'm afraid of death.

Immortality is closed, she said. No need to fear death.

What then? He didn't understand. He didn't want to be Don Quixote. Like Sancho Panza, he wanted to keep one foot in reality. Quixote denounced the romance novels in the end. The age of chivalry was dead.

"I tilted at windmills when I was young," he said.

Yes, you did.

"We fought the good battles, for justice, to end wars, to feed the hungry . . ."

I'm proud of you, she said.

"Yes, but some memories make me sad."

That can't be helped. From experience the brain creates memoires. Experience and remembering, that's life. Quit tilting at old stuff— go out and create new memories!

"Like Don Quixote?"

Be yourself, she said, and leaned to kiss his forehead, like Dulcinea had kissed Don Quixote in the movie.

"Yes!" the old man cried out. "Create new memories! Thank you!"

A Bargain

The Angel of Death approached God with a deal. Some say God listened. In those days all angels were equal, so God had nothing to fear.

"What do you want now?" God asked. He was busy.

"Have I got a deal for you!"

"Yeah?"

The angel got up close. "Listen to this. If you allow humans to experience death and grief, I will give them two other gifts."

"Like what?" God asked.

The old man was thinking he didn't like the smell of this. But he wanted to see where it was going, so he kept writing.

"I will allow them to think for themselves and to enjoy sex."

"Think and have sex," God murmured. His creations were new on earth, so none had yet died from the touch of this angel, who was dressed in white robes and exuded a sweet perfume.

"Go on," God said. He was curious.

"Think of it. Humans will be able to build great civilizations, art works, symphonies to soothe the soul, turn rivers from their rightful courses, fly to the moon. Someday they will invent cars, mobile phones, the internet! They will thank you!"

"Hmm." God was interested.

"And during sex they will experience that 'little death' when time stands still. They will soar to the heavens during those brief moments, thanking you. They will have children, and think they will live forever in their offspring. That's where I come in."

"How?"

"Living forever is a fallacy. All must eventually die."

"Not sure I understand," God said.

Maybe he hadn't thought of death. There was no death in the garden, only eternal blooming. Besides, with so many galaxies flying around the exploding universe, he was beginning to wonder if the Big Bang was a good idea. Why were dark matter and dark energy filling up the universe? He kept checking his equations. On top of everything, Lucifer was revolting.

"They'll love you for it," the Angel of Death said.

"But they must die?" God asked.

"Nobody lives forever. That's the deal."

"Okay, okay," God agreed. "I gotta go. Bye!"

The Angel of Death smiled and went to work.

Death was incorporated into human nature, and because *Homo sapiens* could now think, they became aware of loss and its toll. The rest of nature was indifferent. In fact, Mother Nature laughed at the humans' new predicament. Why weren't they content to live like the rest of the natural world? Seasons come and go and nature doesn't feel loss. Things just are.

For humankind, sex became a driving force by which to begat and begat, and that was fine— the species thrived. That was part of the bargain.

Can't have your cake and eat it too, the old man thought.

He was writing a story, "Last Exit to Aztlán." It wasn't going well. Young Chicanos no longer read the legends of the homeland. Few read the history of their ancestors. In fact, most of the young had already exited, right into the arms of mega-corporations. Make money and get ahead was the new mantra.

The rich were getting richer and the poor poorer. A revolution was brewing, nations colliding against each other like galaxies spun out of their orbits, and the powerful and moneyed sat on high, just enjoying the show.

Books had gone out of style, or were being censored and burned by narrow political ideologues. A new fascism was on the rise; I'm right, everybody else is left out. My way or the highway!

Maybe I should publish on the internet, go viral, the old man thought. He still preferred print books.

A new technology had evolved, the new dynamo of contemporary transcendentalists. Power! A new history! But who was in control? Who was writing history?

Power to the people! some shouted.

Don't be fooled, the old man wrote. The masses suffer at the bottom. It ain't your history that gets taught at school.

The angel's gift— every person thinking for himself or herself. Me first. Individualism has trumped community. What happened to compassionate humanism?

The old man shook his head. Had the angel pulled one over on God?

Thanksgiving

He opened his eyes. He was sitting in the rocking chair; he had fallen asleep.

Had someone spoken? His wife?

No, it was his own voice he had heard. Was he dreaming? It didn't matter. Words had sound, thoughts sounded only in the mind. That's why nobody could tell what anyone was thinking. Either way, words, like thoughts, disappeared. Words and thoughts were faster than the speed of light, evaporating into the world's atmosphere. Did they really disappear? Did words and thoughts continue streaming into the far-flung universe, perhaps to be picked up by antennas in distant galaxies?

Eventually, black holes in the universe would swallow all matter and light.

Then what? The God particle?

Words and thoughts, thus the joys and tragedies of human experience, were briefly recorded, then disappeared.

There were too many words in the life of an old man. Too many promises, some he had kept, some he broke. Too many indiscretions. Growing old meant he remembered all the stupid things he did in times past.

Damn the muse of memory!

He closed his eyes again. Sometimes when he dozed, half asleep or half awake, he could hear her. He listened intently. Donde estás? he asked. Where are you? He asked that a lot lately. Was dying the same as disappearing?

He remembered the *Howdy Doody Show* he had watched on TV as a kid. Howdy Doody said kawabunga. What did it mean?

Am I reverting? Old people revert, he knew. They lose it. Hear voices. Voices from long ago. An infinity stored in memory.

Words created images out of old experiences. Or images created words? Which came first, the chicken or the egg?

Say love and an image jumps up. Maybe not if the brain is clogged. I think, therefore I am. I forget, therefore I ain't.

Men think greed or envy or war and go out and act on their thoughts. I think war, therefore I make war. I want to possess all the wealth in the world, therefore I go get it. Ideas of becoming a superman prevailed, screwing up humanity.

Day and night, the brain churned out a stream of continuous memories. Memories became mind, a kind of consciousness that briefly saw the light then flowed back into the dark pit of the unconscious. Was the unconscious the black hole of the mind? Memories were images, brief pictures stored in the brain; sooner or later they disappeared into that black hole.

Sooner or later everything disappeared.

Still, the flow of images, those hieroglyphics scratched on brain cells, kept flowing across the old man's fevered mind. Memories from long ago fell to the floor and piled up around the rocking chair. Like so many wasted days and wasted nights.

The old man had a cold. It had gotten into his bones and just wouldn't leave. Sneezing. His sinuses plugged up, that awful feeling. It wasn't the cold that bothered him, it was the day, Thanksgiving.

He thought of family as they used to gather in the old days, enjoying all that came with the feelings of warmth and love. His wife was a great cook. God, she could cook. A good meal can cure almost any ailment, she often said.

Now thoughts of food kept rising then falling away, like the ebb and flow of waves crashing against a dark and rocky shore. Food for him? No, he was thinking about his wife's last Thanksgiving meal. What did she eat that day? Their last Thanksgiving together. He couldn't remember.

This was his first Thanksgiving alone. He hadn't thought about it until after his morning coffee and a boiled egg. He felt the silence in the house heavier than usual. He cleaned the kitchen and paid some bills. The morning wore on, and no one called. It wasn't till noon, that time when families gathered for the noon-day meal, carving a turkey, the table laden with pumpkin pies, the kitchen full of laughter, a TV tuned to a football game, that he realized no one was coming.

They had invited him, but being in other people's homes didn't feel right, so he begged off.

Someone had told him holidays were the hardest. The warning hadn't registered, but now he felt it. The sense of loss was building, becoming emotion, something heavy in his chest.

Sadness, just call it sadness.

If only he could remember what his wife had eaten last Thanksgiving. If he could remember the meal he had served her maybe that would somehow lessen the sense of aloneness he felt.

Is that what it was? Loneliness. Mourning for her, for himself. Mourning becomes the old man.

Grief was not a thought he could control, it was an emotion. He knew that, and he also knew that not even the damnedest fool on earth could control emotions— they had their own energy and came and went as they pleased.

He tried to concentrate: their last Thanksgiving together, then her decline. She would last a month.

So food became important. He had thought that if he could keep feeding her she would last. Nourishing her. Every morning he got out of bed, helped her to the bathroom, then went to the kitchen to start the coffee.

It had become a satisfying routine. He helped her from the bathroom to her chair then hurried to start breakfast. He got quite good, he told himself, at making hot cereal, a soft-boiled egg and toast. The trick was for everything to be ready at the same time.

She could still feed herself then, but that would change as the sun dipped into the December solstice. After that he had fed her, sitting by her and coaxing her to take small spoonfuls of cereal, a sip of coffee or milk. Some mornings one of the daughters would stay from work to help.

She had looked at him and thanked him. She'd smiled. Sometimes he had to look away from the wisdom in her eyes. Wisdom and love. She had known what was coming.

"You take such good care of me," she had said.

How could it be otherwise? In him there was more love than wisdom. He didn't know how difficult the eventual end would be.

She began to turn away from even meager bites of food. No amount of coaxing could get her to eat. The cereal grew cold on the tray, the milk untouched.

Worry became a companion. More like dread, a dark, sad shadow deep in the primitive part of the old man's brain. A keening cry erupted in the night as he tossed and turned in bed. He would awaken, go quietly to her room, and peer in. A daughter slept in a cot near the hospice bed. Already angels swarmed the room, flying from across the Jordan, preparing to lift her soul.

Eventually, the only nourishment she would use lay embedded in her flesh.

That's what the nurse who came twice a week told him, always whispering, afraid she would hear. As she takes in less food, the body uses its reserves . . . you have to be ready.

Nourishment. Of body and soul. Perhaps the book he had been writing, the story inspired by her last days on earth, hinged too much on the spirit. The spirit also needed food.

But damn! It was Thanksgiving Day and all he could think about was what she had eaten this day a year ago.

The old man stirred, the chair rocked, the dogs looked up from where they lay on the floor in warm rays of streaming sunlight. What, master? Why did you move? Dreaming? The master was not feeling well. It had been like this since the woman they loved left them.

The old man got up, went into the kitchen, and fed them.

"Wish it was turkey," he said. The dogs didn't mind. Just being with the master was enough.

He peered in the refrigerator. There was stuff he could heat. A bag of chicken wings from last week, beans his sister had brought, wilting lettuce.

Nothing seemed appetizing.

Hell, he could always eat boiled eggs. An old man could live on boiled eggs. If you farted there was no one around.

The old man smiled. But he did need companionship. The day-long silence in the house was too much to bear.

"It's Thanksgiving Day, for crying out loud! Where's the turkey! Red chile and mashed potatoes! Pumpkin pie!"

The words bounced around the kitchen, dull echoes.

He went to her photograph. A frown furrowed her forehead. She wasn't smiling.

"Even an old man needs nourishment!" he cried.

The Garden

Someone is missing from my life . . .

He kept repeating, sing-song, a mantra, repeating, filling the vacuum he felt inside. Does good to repeat things when you're old. That way you don't forget. Of course, he still forgot. A beautiful image would play across the synapses of his brain and he would say, I have to remember that. Use it in the story I'm writing.

But neurons went dead, images and words disappeared. Electrical impulses that would never see the light of day, circuits getting cold.

Brain cells flashed images without rhyme or reason, and some were so clear he could see himself standing there, at the edge of the memory looking in.

His young friend who drowned at Park Lake that summer day of long ago. He could still see everything as if it were just happening. The body came tumbling out of the deep water, floating in slow motion, turning like a dead fish, gold scales shining.

Why did some events remain so clear?

After his own swimming accident, he had spent a summer in the hospital. He remembered the kids in the boy's ward, all crippled by a variety of diseases. One was shriveled by polio, and he lay like a fallen angel in an iron lung. The memory was so clear it made the old man sigh.

Dusk at the river, he heard the terrifying cry of La Llorona, the Crying Woman rushing to snatch him away.

Sunsets on the Mazatlán, sounds of love, their home in Jemez . . . faces. So many faces from the past, now furrowed with age.

Maybe those flashes of insight were caused by sugar spikes in the brain, like a dope high. The LSD experiments of the fifties had at least caused doctors to look closer at the brain's composition. How did that bicameral organ create love?

The brain was a crucible of electric currents, chemicals, and proteins, and this meager stuff created emotions. The Great Mystery at work, the brain recording electromagnetic waves from the furthest galaxies.

Was grief the result of a chemical imbalance? If so, the doctor could give him a shot. Fix it.

"I don't think so," the old man said.

So he shared his thoughts with her. Poetic words. Memories. Songs. Old melodies. I sing along and add my own phrases. Metaphors that help explain what life is all about. Life is a metaphor. Here, there, now here, now there.

Am I the only man in history to have these sudden insights? Epiphanies. Flashes of genius. Ego.

Bull! I'm no Einstein! All in our philosophy has already been writ. Or thought. Or dreamt.

Dreams and thoughts are elusive. If I don't rush and write them down, I forget. They evaporate into an atmosphere of a greater thought. Thought with a capital T. Maybe there's a universal world of Poetic Thought out there. God is Thought. Maybe that's heaven.

The universe is conscious, she said. Consciousness implies thinking.

Yeah, but does the universe remember its beginning? Was there a conscious thought before the Big Bang?

Does it have memory? she asked. We don't know. I do know you're tuned in to some kind of world soul. Your visions.

That's the way it was. She knew because she, too, felt the world soul.

Did the dinosaurs think in poetry?

All creatures are precious and beautiful.

Precambrian? Turtles emerging from the wine-dark sea? The mystery of nature. Yesterday the frogs at the pond were mating. Frog love.

Love belongs to all creatures, and to all the prophets of the world.

A world soul of poetry binds us together. I like that. A glowing golden ribbon. From my belly button to yours. And to all the bellies in the world, before and after.

Can the cord that binds us break?

No, she whispered. Our bond of love was cast at the beginning of time. It has existed since the universal fire began its evolution. "Lovers forever" means whatever was made in that singular instance will last forever. We came spiraling into the universe.

"Ah, damn," he groaned. A joyful pain filled his heart. She had beautiful ways to describe their love. Tears filled his eyes.

Hush, she said. Don't let the poetry of love sadden you.

He wiped his eyes. Okay. I'll make notes.

He made notes, then misplaced them. They cluttered his desk. Hundreds of notes on scratch pads, but no way to tell which belonged where. The poems were thoughts floating away into the universal poetic soul.

The most beautiful poetic thoughts are not written. They're lost to this world.

That's the way it is, she said.

He remembered her saying that phrase the night she lay dying. Her eyes had stared into a profound distance, out there, beyond the stars, into the all-together. He turned to look. What did she see?

Her face glowed, beatific. She had spoken a truth. Her words touched chords in his soul. He felt joy, a kind of understanding.

"Did you hear?" he had asked the daughter who stood nearby, keeping vigil.

"What?"

"The meaning of her life revealed, all that she experienced and a sense of where she's going."

That's the way it is said it all. Why search further?

She saw something. What? Something beautiful on the horizon. Like when one sees a brilliant sunset and is drawn into the breathless instant. Not the subject viewing the object, but a blending. The subject becoming lost in the beauty nature offers. The viewer becoming the sunset.

Like the orgasm of love when Lover and Beloved become one.

Charged with the grandeur of God.

Becoming one with God.

That was love.

Yes. Becoming one with the sunset was becoming God. Standing breathless in the beauty of a pristine mountain stream was becoming God. Seeing a soaring eagle with a fish in its talons was becoming God. The humble sparrow drinking at the fountain is God. Bacteria and viruses, good or bad, are God. This earth is God and we are intrinsic in it.

God is stuck in everything, he said.

That's the way it is.

Does a dying person finally see into the true nature of things? The universal truth. God is not a face, but truth and beauty. Self-creating, reverberating throughout the universe, a fire burning in the tiger's eyes. Physics. Exactitude? Or randomness? Both. All those little particles in the universe come into being and never burn out. Light survives, soul survives.

Where is the universe going?

Where are we going?

Soul survives and soul is creativity. Soul adapts. The soul inhabiting the self is creative. Pure imagination. The soul of the universe is creative, constantly growing into its potential.

Is that what she saw the night she died? Or did she see someone waiting to receive her? Calling to her from beyond the veil? The welcoming hands of her parents, grandparents, her grandmother Eva, ancestors reaching out to take her hand. The veil itself only a thin mist, the stuff of imagination.

The old man had written that one's ancestors waited on the other side. Spirits. One cast off the body and went to visit them. They waited. There was reunion. Love continued to thrive. There was no end to love and soul.

Or was there?

What had she seen?

Had it been only an acceptance that her life was ending?

As a young man he had suffered a spinal cord injury. Diving into the river, he fractured a vertebra. Paralysis was instant and complete. He could not move. Face-down, he had floated up to the surface, but he couldn't turn over to breathe. He was going to drown.

It was then he saw his soul rise into the blue sky. It rose and he looked down at himself floating face-down in the water. From above, he saw his friends calling and entering the water. The color of the water and sky turned a golden hue. He smiled. In a moment he would have to suck water into his lungs and drown.

That's the way it was. That's the way it happened.

Something had separated from his body and risen up in a column of light. His essence. Alma. Ánima. Because of his Catholic upbringing he had learned those words. His mother taught him about las ánimas benditas. She prayed to the blessed souls of the departed. They were out there.

Alma, the Spanish word for soul. Some words more poetic than others, but whatever the language, words struggled to describe the transcendent.

Words, like bread, were sacred.

Just in time his friend Eliseo had grabbed him by the hair and pulled him out of the water. He gasped for breath, sucking in the air of life. They rushed him to a hospital, where he lay for months, learning life anew.

What he had experienced that day stayed with him the rest of his life. He survived the paralysis and moved on.

Then she came calling his name. It was their destiny to meet. She found him.

I'm glad I found you, he said.

I was never far away, she answered. Love stories are forever.

Out of the river endlessly rocking, out of the burning desert, heights of the majestic mountains, thunder of rainstorms, the sun's diurnal journey, moon cycles of love, spiraling stars, endlessly seeking each other. Eternal.

The spirit world was vast! The soul did not die, and it could be preserved in an image. Many old cultures understood this. Across time, artists had painted pictures on cave walls and carved stone statues. Egyptian priests at Karnak had prepared mummies for the soul's return. In all cultures the ancestors were worshipped, candles lit, incense burned, prayers chanted . . .

She's in the photograph, he thought. Her image holds her soul! I should have known! The idea hit him with sudden clarity— if he placed enough of her photographs in a circle, he could draw her down! He hurried into the house, stumbling, out of breath, filled with promise.

Very Large Array

The old man searched throughout the house, gathering all her photographs: the ones on his desk, in the bedroom, and the large one on the buffet. He needed more, but there wasn't time to make copies.

The idea had come in a flash and he needed to act right away. Time was like that— it, too, could disappear, he knew.

"Maybe, just maybe," he muttered, "this might work."

He had tried other things, speaking to her daily and awaiting a response, calling her name in the garden. At night he went to sleep thinking of her, whispering her name so she might appear in his dreams, asking the saints to take care of her.

One night she had appeared at the side of the bed. A shadow, reassuring him, but saying nothing. He sat up and looked into the dark, silent bedroom. Nothing. Was it a dream?

Outside the wind blew and scuttled dark clouds across an empty sky.

Now he had this idea and if it didn't work, then what was there to do? He was afraid of going deeper into introspection. A man could get lost in the world of self-thought. And maybe that's all there was anyway, solipsism.

Once upon a time they had visited every part of the state, exploring the natural wonders, learning the mysteries locked in the land where they dwelt. They slept at Chaco Canyon one night, next to a small campfire, over them the breathless, immense sky dotted with God's silver coins. The deserted, ominous pueblo lay still in the violet night. Home of a prior culture. Ancient songs and drumming echoed off the cliffs.

Something happened here, thought the old man.

In the distance coyotes called.

He remembered Machu Picchu with its massive, precisely cut stones. At Chaco the stonework was delicate, reflecting the tenuous hold the desert had on its people.

This is our Stonehenge, he whispered.

Yes, she said. I remember the morning we drove from Avebury to Stonehenge. The monoliths were enveloped in morning mist, the mystical aura those people had left behind. I feel it here. Those who once lived here had aligned the sun and the moon's cycles into their homes and ceremonies. A true relationship with nature and the cosmos.

In the morning, the New Mexico sun cut like a dagger across the desert, a summer solstice swathe of light. Life in balance.

They walked through the ruins. For these two in search of ancient knowledge, Chaco Canyon was more than an archaeological site, it was a pueblo alive with a spiritual presence.

A breeze rustled the dry grass. A raven called, its shadow passing over the two, followed by a large hawk that struck the raven dead. A mystery.

One October on their way to Bosque del Apache they had visited the Very Large Array of antennas spread across the desert near Socorro. Huge dish-like radio antennas pointed at outer space. The dishes received radio waves from the farthest galaxies and funneled them into computers.

Radio astronomy studied black holes, nebulae, the very beginnings of the Big Bang. The antennas could pick up celestial objects that emitted radio waves.

Electromagnetism, the third force of the universe.

The spirits of Chaco Canyon, the fourth force.

Did scientists secretly hope to receive greetings from life in outer space? Perhaps a disc jockey in a faraway galaxy playing rock 'n' roll songs? Elvis singing be-bop-a-lula in a parallel universe?

The old man smiled. What if the spirit world is a parallel universe? Alive next to us, but we can't see it. Full of spirits emitting soul energy.

He began to wonder. If those radio antennas could find celestial objects, could he find his celestial love? His Beloved. Were there currents of electromagnetism in the heart? The electric flow of love between them. Yes, there were!

The idea of an antenna is obvious, he thought. That's how his television worked. A dish on top of the house received transmissions from a satellite and fed them to a receiver connected to his TV set. He could watch old cowboy movies beamed down from high above the earth.

"Beam me up, Scotty."

He would beam her down! Her photographs would be the antenna. A dozen of her images would call her down!

He had begun to deny the panic he felt, could not admit that he was trying too hard. It has happened to others whose grief sent them spiraling out of control— they went to mediums, entered hypnosis, got religion, kept journals where they recorded the voices they heard, traveled to Sedona or Taos to look into crystals. Some went crazy into sex and booze. All suffering grief, all hoping to communicate with the departed.

A human need.

Charlatans preyed on the need that he felt. They promised to contact the loved one on the other side. They wrote books, conducted séances, swore they had been taken up by UFOs, told believers they would be raptured up to their loved ones. All for a price. Profitable industries developed, all promising relief from sorrow.

"Not for me!" the old man said. "I'll do it my way."

He tore through closets looking for photos. Family parties, weddings, travel pictures, gathering any that held her image. Breathing hard, hands trembling, he clutched a dozen or so photos close to his chest and hurried to the den. The room was circular, like a kiva. Sacred space.

He placed the photographs in a circle and sat in the middle. He felt exhausted, but satisfied. "Why didn't I think of this before?" he whispered.

Chamisa jumped on the couch to nap; Oso came to sit by him, always faithful. The old man hugged his friend. The two sat quietly, waiting for her to appear. He thought he felt her presence.

"Got to concentrate," he whispered to the dog.

I'm here, she said, reaching for him, but unable to touch him. Search no further.

He didn't hear.

"I didn't take my medicine this morning," he remembered aloud. He felt light-headed. Was he trying too hard to reach her? Not listening to his heart?

He studied her face in the photographs. One showed her at fifteen, a slender beauty in a bathing suit. By high school, her face glowed with intense expectations. She had already decided on freedom, a free will. Later, a lovely, noble face with long, dark hair. When she started teaching she cut her hair shorter. In all the photos, her lovely blue eyes looked out at him. Her hair went gray, her smile remained, her inner strength never diminished.

Kindness and nobility, welcoming all who came to their home.

You're here!

Yes.

In the photographs?

In you, she whispered.

Forgive me, he said.

She smiled. All was forgiven.

Lord, he thought. We have to learn to forgive. Perhaps that was the only lesson learned from aging. Compassion.

The hours ticked away. The sun shone through the large plate-glass window, blue sky and scurrying clouds, green top of pear tree.

He heard himself praying, old prayers he had learned as a child. Prayers to the goddess, the Virgin.

Awareness disappeared . . . he entered a stupor ruled over

by songs and poems that rose from old memories. Speaking in tongues, each whispered mantra praising her name. He kept asking her to step out of the spirit world and into the circle where he sat.

Memories, image after image, bubbled up from old brain cells. All the good times, then the days she lay in bed, dying. That final night he had held her hands, kissed her over and over and told her it was time for her heart to stop beating, her breath to grow still.

She had smiled, closed her eyes, and stepped into the night eternal.

Long-lost thoughts exploded in his brain, synaptic connections and neurons flashing electricity, erasing them. Remember? the muse of memory asked him over and over. No sequence or order to the muse's questions, just torment.

Do you have any regrets? he had asked his wife one winter afternoon. The garden lay dormant, Persephone sleeping. The pomegranates hanging on the tree were split with ripeness, exposing red seeds.

No, she answered. What's done is done.

How many can say they have no regrets when their sun is setting? He remembered feeling comforted. But then her strength had always been his anchor.

Now, he felt a sensation, something vibrating. He opened his eyes. He had fallen asleep, legs cramped, kidneys aching.

I need water, but I can't leave now.

Suppose a scientist on duty at the Very Large Array had turned off the electricity to take a toilet break. While he was gone a voice from outer space spoke: "Hello Earth, do you hear me?" The voice waited, and when Earth didn't answer, the voice moved on to other galaxies, searching for signs of life. It made a note: "No life on Earth."

I can't take a chance, the old man thought. Can't leave.

The circle of photographs shimmered, light reflected off her face, her smile made him tremble.

Was she coming alive?

"Hijita," he whispered, reaching for her. The room swirled, a vortex, round and round, making him dizzy. He groaned, closed his eyes, called her name. It was working, he was going into a trance. He could see her gliding across the garden, down the hollyhock path, and into the circle. She would sit by him.

You're home, he said.

Silly man, I was always home.

He raised his arm to take her hand, but instead fell face down. He let out a cry that frightened the dog. It moved away, observing the master with curiosity, perhaps a bit of fear.

"Got to stay awake," the old man mumbled. "Got to keep calling her."

Every bone in his body hurt. The room grew hot. He knew he was passing in and out of consciousness. The vibrations increased; he felt the earth trembling.

Then the mercy of God struck the firmament— clouds scuttled across the sky, darkening the room, too late for the old man who lay unconscious on the floor. An old, limp scarecrow, a bag of bones, drying to a crisp.

Night soon arrived, cool as always in the desert land.

She came with a blanket and covered him. She sat by him and waited. He was dying. He had found her.

The Gloom

He gave it a home: the gloom.

It came unexpectedly, the sadness. Sometimes after family or friends had been by to visit, maybe after a nice dinner, good conversations, a pleasant evening— then they left.

"Bye."

"Take care."

"Call us if you need anything."

"See you later, gator!"

A silence would settle throughout the house. The old man sat in his rocking chair, the dogs settled to sleep on the floor.

The afternoon sunlight, bright as that which drenched Toledo the day they were there, now turned the Spanish broom in the garden a brilliant van Gogh yellow. The lace vine shone white as a bride's veil. The hollyhocks of late May had burst open. A silence seeped through the garden, and he remembered the cry of peacocks in León. He had stood on the terrace. In the garden of the parador the peacocks cried, león, león— the mournful cries of women whose sons rested in that battered earth.

"The gloom," he said aloud. The dogs looked up, sharing a silent communication with him.

The dogs missed the woman who had taken such good care of them. Now the old man fed them and made sure their water bowl was always full. They followed close at his side, perhaps afraid the master, too, might disappear.

Did they wonder if she would return? She who had always taken such good care of them. She who was full of kindness.

The old man's niece and her husband came that morning.

"I fell asleep," the old man explained, his voice breaking with disappointment. She hadn't come, he hadn't been able to draw her down.

In the kitchen he gulped down glasses of cold water. His hands shook.

While he showered, they gathered the photographs and the blanket. They asked no questions, but they wondered, what was he doing? Had he slept on the floor? Was he losing it?

They didn't know the weight that filled his heart. He had thought he could make her appear, speak to her, perhaps have her on earth again. It was not to be.

Maybe I am going crazy, the old man thought. The experiment with the photographs was ridiculous. He had to accept that.

The following day he decided to plant a tree. Replace one that died. His nephew drove him to a nursery, they bought a tree, and planted the young sapling in the front patio.

"For you," he said when they were done. She loved redbud trees. Now she had two.

He had the instincts of a farmer. One plants a tree even if he may not be around to see it bloom the following spring. But planting the tree didn't dispel the gloom he felt. Something was bothering him. What?

Was he just imagining her? Was it all in the imagination? Was the presence he felt only his wish for her to be with him? For her to be as she used to be . . .

A wish, his desire, but all inside him, locked in memories. She wasn't out there, she was in him. That's what she kept telling him.

Realizations were condensing into a new way to think about the spirit world. Could he go there?

Since her death all he did was think of her. Every moment, around every corner. Constantly talking to her, believing she was reachable. To touch her, to hear her voice, to have her approval, to share daily details, his visit to the pond, the store, evening sunsets, clouds, a spring breeze sweet with her perfume.

Were memories the only thing left? Was the gloom he felt a realization she now lived only in his memory?

Still, he kept asking, Where are you? He needed answers.

Maybe he should find someone who might understand what he was going through. A woman he could talk with, call on the phone— conversations to kill the gloom.

Instead, he talked to the dogs, slowly coming to understand that he wasn't taking care of them, they were caring for him.

"She told you to take care of me, didn't she?"

They jumped with excitement, their intelligent eyes answering him. The master needed companionship! They were all he had. He began to take pleasure in their joy.

The old man also talked to himself. He worried. His mind churned all day and into the night. He guessed all those who had lost a loved one were in the same boat, talking with the departed.

What could cure this?

The question of him marrying had come up. His sister had mentioned it.

"No," he said. "I don't think so."

But he thought about it. A woman would dispel the loneliness, fill the house with her voice, her laughter, lie in bed with him at night, that loneliest of times. Yes, he needed a woman, someone who cared for him. Desire? Love? Was it too late?

He read that stars and planets affected each other's gravity. Push and pull. Massive stars ten times bigger than the earth's sun curved the fabric of space-time. The body was like a planet bending time until the person went spiraling down. He was spiraling down, lost in a vast space, unable to feel the gravity of those who circulated nearby.

Maybe a woman would pull him back into a steadier orbit.

Se acaba la cuerda, his neighbor said, an old hispano who had grown up in the folkways of nuevo mexicano culture. The springs wind down. The body is a clock whose springs propel the hours, days, months, years, until the clock stops, never to go again.

Does the soul also wind down?

One day while they were sitting together, he had asked her how she felt. "I'm going south," she had told him. Of the four directions, she had chosen south to mean the land of the departed. Now the old man felt he was going south. Sooner or later everybody went south. Some mornings he didn't have the energy for life.

When they were young they had been like two giant stars drawn into each other's gravitational fields, circulating in perfect rhythm, dancing epicycles around each other, stupendous sunbursts and galactic rainbows of love, creating a harmony that echoed the ancient songs of the celestial spheres.

Now, thinking of a new woman coming into his life, he wasn't sure. Too old to marry. Besides, he was still married to the woman whose ashes rested in the urn on the fireplace mantel. Still married to her spirit.

He had gone out with an old acquaintance, but it didn't work. He felt no pull of love. Was there a woman in the star-filled horizon who could bend him to her gravitational pull? Could he ever orbit around a great love again? Would he ask too much of a relationship? Could love thrive in the time of going south?

He was getting used to being alone, used to the silence. What would a woman say about his gloom? A new star would not come as a virgin, a tabula rasa on whose soul he might inscribe his desires. No, a woman would come with her own habits, idiosyncrasies, likes, dislikes, tastes. There were plenty of widows out there, but each would come with baggage from her former marriage, kids and grandkids, friends, home, everything. She would come replete with memories of her prior life. Too many mixed emotions.

Was there space in his universe for a new star? Could his weakened gravity engage a new moon?

No, it wouldn't work.

He didn't want to trap anyone into taking care of him. Eventually, an assisted living home could do that. Maybe one wife had been enough. Their marriage had not ended because she died. Divine marriages didn't end.

But why the gloom?

He had been talking to her all day, thinking of her, drawn here and there by memories. Depression? Yes, a feeling of helplessness was constant. He had given up seeing friends, hid his depression from family. Never mentioned it, never told anyone that at times sadness became gloom.

He had talked to a grief counselor, a young woman who left a few pamphlets for him to read. The visit didn't satisfy, so he decided to tough it out on his own. He found it difficult to express his sense of loss to others.

Maybe join a group where he could sit quietly in the back row and listen to others. He needed to do something, so he had resolved to become more active. He wrote letters to old friends, paid bills that had piled up, walked every morning to the park, enjoyed visits with his niece and her husband, who looked after many of his needs. Once a week he ate dinner with the daughters, and had lunch with his sister, who brought his favorite New Mexicans foods. To all, he appeared to be in his right mind.

Did they sense the gloom in him? Is that why they called to check on him? His sister called every day.

"How are you? How was your day?"

"I'm fine. Yeah, had a good day."

"Okay, just checking."

They didn't know he lived with a ghost, her spirit, his Beloved. She lived in him. Everything seemed to exist in him. Did the spirit world also live in him? In his memory?

Is that what it was coming to?

Had he found the spirit world within?

As long as he remembered those who had died, they lived in memory. Grandparents, parents, brothers, sisters, his wife. All in his memory.

During this time others died: an older sister, then a great-nephew, a former colleague, a childhood friend, recently a brother in-law.

All the good people gone, living now only in his memory.

The Hospital

The old man sat on the porch, wine glass in hand. He sipped, let the liquid wash over his palate, tasting and giving thanks. He held the glass up and watched the ruby red colors scintillate in the streaming sunlight. He swirled the wine and breathed deeply its fragrance.

"Gracias a Dios," he whispered.

He looked at the clouds. The Cloud People were not rising as giant cumulus today, but lay flat between two atmospheric levels. The Sky People floating along a sky corridor.

Soft mauve clouds glowed with apricot-colored edges, as if an artist had rubbed crayons into paper, leaving the color embedded. Red crayon and paper became the red lips of the woman he painted. Which was real? The paper, the color, or the image the viewer perceived as a woman with red lips?

Transformations. The clouds would condense, become drops of rain, become rivers, then become clouds again. What lasted? Flor y canto, the ancient Aztecs had written. That's all that lasts, beauty of flowers and songs.

With so much illusion in this world, he had to believe in beauty and truth. Was the next world also an illusion? What truly lasted beyond the flow of space and time?

A change was in the air. That morning an early October rain had washed out the Albuquerque Balloon Fiesta. Undaunted, the tourists headed for Old Town to eat Mexican food and buy Indian jewelry.

In the garden, dew on the bushes glistened in the morning light. God was the light shining on the green leaves. God was light, and even light moved away, changed, created shadows upon shadows until the night cometh. Nothing held still.

The people of the valley rejoiced. The dry earth thanked the rain. Every drop was a blessing from the Cloud People.

That prior week the old man had been in the hospital for a series of tests.

Doctors love to test, he thought. You get old and they start poking you for this disability or that, new prescriptions, call in the specialists, injections, lab work. Blood analysis told them all they wanted to know.

When they removed the IV needle, a vein had exploded in his arm. The bruise will go away, the doctor said. The old man's arm remained dark purple for weeks. The color of death. Unsettling.

Where is the joy and passion we once knew? The exhilaration of youth.

Attendants and nurses at the hospital were friendly. He met some caring people, but the experience had not been good. Pushed and pulled from one lab to another, his ass showing through the gowns they made patients wear. Degrading.

Through the open door of his sick room he had watched other patients walk the hall. The sick, walking back and forth like lost souls. They had lost their freedom. He swore he didn't want to end like that.

No freedom for old men, he thought. Old men descending. Like Prometheus chained to a bed, nurses' aides poking needles at the liver. A dark labyrinth.

Freedom's just another word—

"It's everything!" he shouted. The dogs looked up. The master had been gone three days. He was not well.

One disability after another took away freedom. Death, the final disability. A new kind of freedom.

I don't want to end up in a hospital tied to a bed, he said to his wife.

A sadness heaved in her chest. What could she do? How could she help him?

I was raised on the Santa Rosa llano, he said. My father and his cowboy friends were an independent breed. They worked hard and drank hard. Muscles of steel. Sky and the open range shone in their eyes, stirred their blood. Freedom bred in the bone.

She reached out, a gesture of love that could not be completed.

You were brave, he said to her. You were so patient during those long days and nights of your hospice. You taught me how to face death. Did I learn? Why this fear?

Because you're not ready, she answered. After a long pause, she added, The time will come, and you will know.

He wanted to understand, but the freedoms he was losing frightened him. Each day a new disability, the worm turning. I need to be here in our home, he protested. The home we built! It's us!

He looked up at the clouds, harbingers of autumn rains. Where will I go? Sooner or later I have to give up our home. Tears filled his eyes.

We have to give up everything, she said, her voice breaking with her desire to comfort him.

Time was running out. The body, clock-like, could not be wound up again. Sure they were making body parts from stem cells, replacement parts, but only up to a point. The body's gravity obeys nature's complement.

"And we all fall down," he hummed.

The hospital stay really knocked me for a loop. I really felt the loss of freedom. I mean, that's all I got left.

There is a way, she said.

"Rage, rage against the dying of the light!" he cried out, startling the dove at the water bowl. A great flutter of wings filled the air, then stillness. The dogs came to sit at his feet.

No, she answered, go gentle. Be ready to enter absolute freedom. Know the time when you come to take my hand.

The old man nodded. If only a person could ask a doctor for the final injection. Be in charge of the last gasp toward complete freedom. There are laws against us being in charge of the final step. We should be the ones to decide.

So we wait, and the freedoms of our youth ebb away. One by one. When one foot is already on the other side of the bar, we should be allowed to cross. Why drag the tortured body through so much pain?

"Should a body meet a body, coming through they rye . . ." To meet her. That's what he wished for.

He looked up.

The clouds lay spread out across the sky like so many angels awaiting their autopsies.

Joy and Passion

The trick is to find joy and passion again.

Trick?

The possibility of finding joy and passion. How to realize those moments again. To experience the joys of life one has to engage life. One can't be passive. The depths of love are not for the idle.

Ah, but he just didn't feel the old urges; a kind of depression had settled in. Introspection, he called it.

The old man stood at the pond, his Walden. Here, a slice of nature was contained within the city. Here abounded a diversity of life.

Why did Mother Nature create so much diversity? Because she doesn't want to die. Thousands of her progeny can be wiped off the face of the earth, but other members of her large family will survive. She knows a calamity is coming and it has nothing to do with the Bible or Mayan prophecies. Man and his bombs will eventually burn away most of the face of the earth, but she will survive.

With the few of her creations that survive Armageddon, she can populate the earth anew. A few seeds here, cockroaches and other insects there, a fish at the bottom of the sea. She'll survive.

Does this mean Mother Nature thinks? She plans for the future?

The old man nodded. His observations told him this was true. The earth was conscious. This knowledge had been realized long ago, and now he also knew.

In the water a large goldfish floated, dead, its once-brilliant scales now gray, mottled with a white film. Its bulging eyes stared skyward, seeming to contemplate the heavens, a gesture of peace.

Does God have a scale to weigh the flesh of the dead fish? Can he weigh all the creatures that have died? Is heaven the universal scale into which everyone fits?

Jackal-headed Anubis, an ancient Egyptian god, weighed the hearts of the dead. The rulers were buried in a tomb and presumably allowed into the pantheon of the elect. The riffraff were buried in the desert sand or tossed into the Nile.

The old man peered into the dark water.

Seven smaller fish, also dead, were suspended on the thin surface. The surface of the water was an illusion. Where sky and water met was called surface, a word describing that which didn't exist.

The belly of the sky touched the water. Why not call the water's surface the belly of the sky? Too many words describing what didn't exist.

The belly of the sky lies on the water, injecting lightning bolts, fire to awaken dormant cells in the mud at the bottom. Life begins anew.

Does love exist beyond the word *love*?

Death had come to the pond. Did desire also die?

The old man's musings saddened him.

Years ago he and his wife had visited China. At first, the workings of the socialist society didn't interest him. He knew little of the political ideology that had organized and changed profoundly that great civilization.

The old man, much younger then, was searching for an ideology of the soul. How does one organize the soul, the essence within that harbors all emotions?

Is there an ideology of love? he asked the Chinese he met.

He studied the Path of the Buddha, and it provided momentary peace and harmony. In the temples his spirit felt renewed. Compassion.

But he left the Buddha Path because he could not negate the desires he felt within. He loved life too much, the nights of love with his wife, the touch of Chinese silk, aromas of food in the markets, and the people. He had stood in awe of the harried millions filling the streets, the tumultuous energy, sweating bodies digging canals, no steam shovels, only men like ants swarming to do the party's work.

He felt compassion for old women bent over in rice paddies, mile after mile, planting rice as they had done for millennia. On the street he greeted old grandmas with bound feet, who smoked cigarettes, watching him and his wife pass by. "We're from New Mexico!" he'd exclaimed, and they had smiled. What the hell did they know about New Mexico? What did he know about China?

"Viva China!" he'd shouted in the smoke-filled streets. I love you! He felt desire, an energy for living! He had taken his wife's hand and they went running down a street to buy oranges. They sat next to the orange vendor's stall and sucked at the fresh orange pulp, dripping juice, in China in 1984, eating oranges in a dark, grimy street. A crowd gathered around them and smiled and clapped.

So he returned to the people, not forgetting the tragic aspects of a misguided ideology that had led leaders to implement a destructive cultural revolution.

When he had left China he wrote, "I am full of desire."

Across the pond a mother duck appeared, three gray ducklings busily following her, swimming into their future on the face of the dark water, the belly of the sky.

Seasons came with death and renewal in their wake. The carp's flesh would sink to the bottom of the pond, become stagnant mud, the stuff of life. Ashes to ashes, he had learned during Ash Wednesdays of his childhood, running with friends to church in the dust storms of spring, receiving sacraments, believing everything. You die with a mortal sin on your soul and you will burn forever! God doesn't forgive! The kids shuddered. Oh, my God! I'm sorry for all my sins! Innocents.

Where were the old man's holy days of obligation now?

One of the ducklings would thrive, fly away, then return to the pond in a future season. A new brood would appear. Cycles.

The old man spoke to his wife, describing the mystery of life he jealously guarded at the pond. Bless the dead and the living and move on.

Can I desire again? he questioned. Can I find joy and passion? Has my season ended?

Ours is not to know the season's final chapter, she cautioned. Walk the path of the sun, sing the songs of the moon. Remember?

Of course he remembered. He had written, She walks the path of the sun, she sings the songs of the moon. The summer sun had tanned her a lovely brown, and she kept the cycles of the moon. Aware of celestial movements, acknowledging their presence in her life.

So it must have been in every culture of the Americas— before popish calendars and French clocks arrived the ancients kept sacred calendars. From Tierra del Fuego and Machu Picchu to Copán, they made signposts, dating back to the beginning in Siberia, the Manchurian steppe. The ancestors plotted cycles of sun, moon, and planets, and the minutes of the revolutions influenced their lives.

Sing a song for me, she whispered. Sing the full moon.

The old man looked east, there where la crónica del alba, the chronicle of dawn, began each day. In that house made of dawn the moon readied herself to rise over the Sandia Mountains. Dressed in a colorful gown of soft pastel wispy clouds, the Grand Lady yawned and rose, destined to be in Alburquerque at this exact moment according to the most ancient calendars.

"Luna," the old man whispered, "I'll sing a song for you!"

He stumbled out into the yard and stared at the full moon rising.

"Damn!" he said. "There's hope. From resurrection springs hope."

He stood in awe as the silver coin of the Great Mystery bathed the Alburquerque Valley in its light, connecting sky to mountain to hollyhocks swaying in the cool breeze. The trumpet vine burst open, announcing the full moon's birth. Hosannah!

Denizens of the city came out of their homes to look. A sense of wonder filled the people. As long as the moon rose there was hope. They called the children. See the man in the moon! Look, Billy!

Look, Susie! See the old man in the moon? The children looked and saw what their parents believed. The face of an old man on the moon.

"No!" the old man shouted. "It's a rabbit imprinted on the face of the moon! Long ago an Aztec god threw a rabbit at the moon and there it is! See?"

Old man or rabbit, people saw what they were taught to see.

The old man heard a drumming, then a flute, women chanting. The Cloud People filled the house made of dawn with their song.

The Mayan calendars had predicted that on this evening at this exact moment, the moon would rise over the Sandia Mountains and the old man would be there to greet it. That's the way it was, that's the way it had always been. Believers greeting the moon goddess.

Your moon, he said, and she smiled.

Sing a song for me, a song of my youth.

Sing a song, moon rising, song of love.

The old man turned and saw her walking toward him, humming. He smiled, took her hand and began to sing.

"A song I am sending,

A song of love I am sending,

Goddess of love."

The huge, round moon rose into the Alburquerque evening sky, shining so brightly everyone shouted with glee.

Everyone from Isleta Pueblo to Bernalillo heard the old man singing. He was dancing on the lawn, crippled as he was, the three-legged man held up by his cane, howling like a coyote for its mate, howling and dancing.

The river coyotes heard his cries and answered. Up and down the river the coyotes yipped at the rising moon, their sharp joyful cries serenading the crazy man on the hill.

The coyotes on the west mesa also begin to sing, sharp cries of joy. There would be no hunting tonight, this was a night for singing and dancing.

This moment had never taken place anywhere on earth before,

unless something like it had happened last month and the month before, but then the old man hadn't been dancing with his wife on the green, sparkling lawn, their feet wet with sweet dew.

The old man's song rolled down the hill, spreading up and down the valley. His howls echoed against the mountain, and soon the entire city was dancing and singing and praising the full moon that had come so far across the calendars of time to grace the people of Alburquerque.

Word of this spread. A miracle, some said. Nowhere else had the moon ever shone as bright and big, unless it was in Palenque long ago. Or on the altars of Giza when Isis and Osiris walked through a moonlit night, Osiris knowing his time on earth was coming to an end. The desert moon had shone on those two lovers as it had shone on Romeo and Juliet, Quixote and Dulcinea, Cyrano and Roxanne. Now it shone on the old man and his wife dancing on the lawn.

Soon people from all over the world were coming to Alburquerque just to be present when the full moon rose over the Sandia Mountains. Lovers vowed love forever, the sick were cured, compassion flourished. If the full moon could be born anew every month, there was hope in rebirth.

Everyone sang and danced and claimed they could hear the howling of the old man on the west mesa, there where he had lived with his wife, whose countenance now shone on the face of the moon, lovely as the day he fell in love with her. He called her name and whirled round and round in a dervish dance until he fell into the arms of the flowers and green grass.

They say people came to visit him— even holy men from India who had washed in the Ganges came, women who could not conceive came to see him, the lame and the sick of heart came. Pariahs and outcasts came. Rich and poor came. The children came.

Year after year, thousands came to see the full moon rising over the Sandia Mountains, because it had been foretold in ancient calendars that love would flourish in its light. The children who loved the earth learned to walk the path of the sun and sing the songs of the moon.

Those nights when the moon shone bright, they could still hear the old man's song echoing down the valley.

"Where is he?" someone asked.

A child answered, "He went away."

The Old Man Got a Girlfriend

Loneliness drove him to call the old classmate he had met at the reunion. He missed intimacy. He phoned her and invited her to lunch at his home.

They talked. He found her interesting, open-hearted, sexy. Especially sexy. Why wait? he thought. He hadn't felt this way in a long time.

He complimented her on her looks, checked out her legs, and felt, for the first time in a long time, there were possibilities.

The way her eyes shone told him she was interested. But in what? Did she need what he needed? I need, you need, we all need. Were the needs true? Or was this a game?

"We are on earth to love—" he thought he heard her say.

We need love! That's the bottom line! Sometimes just touching another person will do. Won't it? What about sex?

At the reunion banquet his knee had brushed against her knee, under the table of course. She had smiled. Ah, she had needs too.

He had to work fast because he didn't know where the whole thing was going. After sandwiches and a glass of wine, he started sweet-talking her. You look good. Forget desert, let me show you the bedroom.

"Hey, you work fast," she said.

"There's so little time left," he said.

"I could come back," she suggested.

"Why wait?"

"I haven't done it since . . ."

She had told him that her husband had died a few years back. So she hadn't done it. Neither had he.

"We're in the same boat," he said, hesitating.

"A ship of fools," she answered.

They laughed.

He practiced a little romantic Spanish on her. "Eres más bella que una rosa." Old stuff like that.

"Ohh." She liked it.

"Lettuce . . . let us go then you and I—"

"What?"

"A piece of lettuce. Stuck between your teeth. Here, like this." He kissed her. "Got it."

"Did not," she said, blushing. "I didn't have lettuce—"

He kissed her again and this time she responded.

"Wow," she said. "I haven't—"

"Since?"

"Yeah."

"Come on. Porqué no? You have to give a little to get a little."

She laughed and pushed him away, gently.

There was hot blood in the old bones, he could feel it. He could taste it on her lips, the way her tongue felt.

Now or never, he thought, took her hand, and hurried her to the bedroom. She knew what was up, but she didn't protest.

"Are you sure?" was all she said.

Oso followed them. "Scat!" the old man shooed. Oso liked to lick toes. Some women didn't like that.

They undressed quickly, she blushing, he laughing nervously. He got her under the sheets and started doing things in a hurry. He was hungry for her. She was what he needed, he guessed.

He thought he heard her whisper, Yes.

So he guessed it was working. Been too long, but once you learn to ride a bike you never forget. He chuckled, a kind of devilish giggle. Satisfaction. He could do it.

But the things he was doing didn't seem to be working. Not like the old days. Had he forgotten how to ride a bike? Was *you never forget* a lie?

Hell, I can do this, he thought. Like long ago. He felt a slight awakening, because she was also trying, she was responding. Her kisses made him dizzy. His senses sputtered alive. You're never too old, he thought. Never forget how to ride— up, down, like this. Don't fall off!

Best not to think of the past. He had to concentrate on what he was doing. Going all the way, the high school boys used to say. Bragging.

Been three years she had told him, sitting next to him at the banquet, his leg rubbing against hers. She was interested.

She whispered a name. "Sorry . . . my husband . . ."

Was she crying? Was he trying too hard?

"It's okay . . . okay."

He understood. She was thinking of the past. Like him. Would they ever be able to let go of the past? The mind played tricks. Maybe the time wasn't right. Would it ever be? He had to find out.

It was their first time together. They hardly knew each other, yet he got her in bed in a hurry. Why?

"Have you?"

"No, not since . . ."

"Me either . . ."

It was a human need. He needed closeness, some kind of comfort. She pulled at him. She needed whatever he was trying to do.

The world had come to be a lonely place. They struggled against loneliness. Was this the way to solve the need, the struggle of love versus loneliness?

"Do you love me?" he thought she asked.

"Yes," he answered. She was trying.

Best not think about it, he thought, just do it. Thinking about sex ruined it. Sex had to be its own thing. He knew that. But that seemed so long ago.

He missed his wife. Her body, her scent, hips, the sweat of their bodies, her warmth and love.

The old man felt confused. The world had somehow slipped away. Had they been trying for a few minutes or an hour? He thought of quitting. He was sweating, breathing hard, but she didn't say stop.

"Like long ago . . ." one of them said, trying to be encouraging.

Felt his heart thumping, for love, he guessed. He worried. The hospital had checked his heart. It was okay. But the stress test on the treadmill was nothing like this.

Things weren't working like they used to. He paused and looked at her. She was lovely. He told her she was lovely, but lovely came out as lonely. Lovely and lonely were a terrible combination, he knew.

Hello loneliness, my old friend . . .

Bingo at the senior citizen center just wasn't cutting it for him. Nor for her. She was hungry too. And lonely. So she had come with him, and he had gotten her in bed in a hurry, and she went along with the play.

She looked at him. "You did good . . ."

He knew she was just being nice. "Yeah?"

It wasn't just sex he wanted. He wanted to care for someone. She knew. They both needed something beyond loneliness. Both needed love. Some kind of love.

Then he was lying beside her, pressing close to her warm body and her scents, and his hunger subsided. He heard a whimper, like a baby makes when he has just fed at his mother's breast. Or when he's still hungry. The old man didn't know if the soft sound came from him or from her. His girlfriend. She was caressing his hair, like a mother runs her fingers across her child's hair.

He ran his hand across her stomach and smiled. Lying close to her was a comfort. Is that what old men needed? Comfort? Hell, his electric blanket was comfort! He wanted something else. What?

The past was past. He knew he couldn't bring back years of sharing, all those nights of passion. Maybe passion was dead. Or he had to figure a new way toward that elusive emotion.

"I love you," he said.

"And I love you," she replied.

They had just met. Things had gotten sudden.

"Carpe diem," he said.

"I guess," she agreed.

"We don't have much time left, so we want it all at once."

"I feel that way," she said.

He felt the tension ease away, like waves from an angry ocean residing, leaving behind a clean, white beach. He wiped his eyes.

"You okay?" he asked.

"Yes," she replied. "You're good. I like being with you."

He smiled. I'm good, huh? I was always good. But I don't know how I got old so quick. Came all of a sudden. I was young and could do anything, then I was old.

"I like being with you," she repeated.

"Think this is love?" he asked.

She laughed softly. "Could be."

"It's our first date."

She smiled. "Like you said, we don't have much time . . ." Her voice trailed off and the old man thought she was crying.

Damn, he thought, I've gone and made her cry!

"Look, let's not talk about time. Let's just enjoy."

She nodded, fumbled for the box of tissues on the nightstand, and blew her nose. "Sorry," she said.

"It's okay. I guess I didn't plan ahead." He paused. "I did get you a box of candy."

She blew her nose again and said, "I'm diabetic."

"I didn't know . . ."

"Ah well, carpe diem."

"Yes. I agree."

Next time get flowers, he thought.

"Are you allergic?"

"To what?"

"Flowers."

"Oh no, I love flowers. I was thinking about what you said. Hay que darle gusto al gusto. I like it when you speak Spanish. More romantic."

"Sí," he answered. "Dar gusto. To give pleasure."

"I guess you just did. Whew."

"La vida pronto se acaba—"

He stopped himself. Why say life soon ends? He had to get away from time and death themes. Love had to be beyond time and death.

"You're sweating."

"I always do . . . when I do this."

She laughed.

"We could try it again," he said.

"Yes, I think. Got to go now. I promised my grandkids."

She covered herself with the sheet and stood.

"I'm shy," she said.

"You look good," the old man said.

"Thanks. My panties?"

"I'll help," he said, getting up slowly. He used to jump out of bed. Long ago. Faded images. He didn't remember when. Now the pain in his lower back and sciatic nerve kept him in check. Old age is a checkmate, he thought.

"Your dog!" she cried. "Look!" She held up the shredded panties. "He chewed a hole in them."

"Oso!" the old man cried out. "Here! Let me—"

"It's okay!" she laughed. "I have a dog. They do these things. It's my fault."

"I'll buy—"

"No, no! I left them on the floor."

Good boy, Oso! the old man thought. Just like his master.

"I'll get—"

"No, no!" She laughed and he laughed with her.

"I haven't had this much fun in a long time," she said, wiping tears from her eyes.

"Really?"

"Yes, really." She kissed him. "I'd like to come back, if . . ."

"I want you to come back, if you . . ."

"When we have more time," she whispered.

"Yes." He felt a bit of joy.

She slipped into her blouse and pants, kissed him, and went quickly out of the room. He heard the front door shut. A domineering silence filled the house.

The old man stood shivering in the afternoon light that poured through the window, casting an aura around his frail body.

He shivered. Forlorn.

Maybe things would work out. Eventually. Best not to hurry. For now, caring was enough. He did care for her, and she would come back.

A ray of light streaked across the floor like a promise.

Letting Go

A thought stirred in the night. Like most random thoughts, it was suddenly there.

It scared him, bad.

"No!" he heard himself cry. "I won't let her go. No, no, no! She's in my heart— my soul mate! That's what we are! As long as I breathe— forever."

In the dark of night, he trembled.

When I die we will lie together, like Beauty and Truth in Emily Dickinson's poem. Do memories exist in the tomb? In the ashes we become? Ah, Emily, wishful thinking.

He sat up in bed, confused.

"What the devil!" How dare his mind conceive of letting her go? A nightmarish voice had spoken. Or indigestion. The cheese he had at dinner— no, he couldn't blame it on a sour stomach.

He got up, walked the floor, drank a glass of water, looked out at the sparkling lights of the city in the valley below, the cusp of a moon barely hanging on in the empty sky. He went to her photograph.

Is that all that's left in the end, photographs? The home we built. Every piece of furniture, books, her voice lingering here and there, favorite foods, friends—

Is everything fading?

He tried to stop thinking. Too many memories! All jumbled up! That was the crux, the memories.

He poured himself a shot of tequila and drank it down. The drink calmed him. He knew a couple of friends who after losing their wives had taken to drinking. To calm the nerves, they said. The old man knew it was because of memories. Bandwagons of good times, emotions unfolding, remembrances of times past.

Now, emptiness. Loneliness.

But letting go of her? Forgetting her? Hadn't he promised her they would be lovers forever? That love note was written in many Valentine's cards over the years. The words would be inscribed on their tombstone. Their ashes would someday rest in a common urn, lovers forever, together at last.

They would walk hand in hand into the night eternal.

Follow your fear finally meant learning to love again. There was no fear but fear itself, and love conquered fear.

Did letting go mean forgetting her? Impossible. The thought had surfaced in the soul's dark night, his subconscious playing dirty tricks.

That's it! he thought. The mind loves to confuse. Too many demons in dark dreams! They can drive one crazy.

The older one got, the more confusion crowded in, and that meant forgetting. So many old people with dementia or Parkinson's. Too much sugar in the diet, the body breaks down, then the mind.

He couldn't blame it on dark thoughts in his primal brain. The voice had been angelic, soothing— hers! Yes, she had spoken.

The thought stayed with him, and he dwelt on it. Was it time to let her go? How could he? Why? Had he reached a crisis point? The thought grew into a certain knowledge, but he wouldn't accept it. Unless it was she who was letting go. Had she come to tell him she was leaving?

If so, how would he fill the Room of Love in his heart?

A week ago he had invited his lady friend to a concert in Santa Fe. Perhaps being in a neutral place they would be more at ease with each other, able to talk, share their respective stories, maybe make love. Not hurried like the first time.

They had driven to a motel, registered, and when he was crossing the patio he'd seen his wife sitting in a garden chair. She had smiled and said, I brought you here.

The vision had startled him. He looked around, saw nothing. What had he seen? Why had she appeared?

He had felt confused, then relieved. She knew his mind, knew his coming and going, so why was he surprised? For visions to have power they had to be acted out for the good of the community. That's why he wrote stories about his visions; the books were the acting out, and if they renewed a person here or there, he had properly used his vision.

He'd told his lady friend what he had seen.

"Something like that happened to me," she said. "My husband appeared and told me to go on with my life."

"That's it," the old man said. "But it's not easy."

"I know," she agreed. "Think how fortunate we are that they come from time to time to bless us."

Then the old man remembered— it had happened one other time.

One evening, soon after she died, he had been sitting alone in the garden. He looked up and saw his wife walking down the hollyhock path. She turned and smiled. He heard her say, I'm going.

An ethereal spirit, walking in beauty in the glowing sunlight. Was she letting go?

He had bowed his head and thanked her, and the gold light moving across the garden fell on his head. She, full of grace and kindness, was blessing the time he had left. That's how he had always understood her appearances.

Her spirit had spoken, he was sure.

But where was she? On a journey into the spirit world, the world of his ancestors? That's how he envisioned the afterlife. Not heaven, Hades, Mictlan, nirvana—where the soul finally escapes the chain of being—Valhalla, the Buddha's bosom, or Hindu dreams. Those concepts belonged to other modes of thought, other religions.

There was nothing new under the sun, he knew, but he had to believe in something, so he imagined the afterlife.

What did anyone really know about the world of spirits? Was it just another name for a place where departed souls hang out? If so, it might as well be heaven. His ancestors, his parents, brothers, and sisters had been good people. They rested in heaven in God's arms.

But the spirit world wasn't a *place*, it was a continuum. Souls didn't die, they became transcendent, became God, the Great Mystery. The departed imbued life, for they were nearby, caring for those left behind.

He prayed to them for guidance.

His wife's soul had wandered into a community of souls, the mourning wind that swept around the earth. A metaphor.

The more he thought, the more he questioned the stories of the prophets that had led him to this point. He questioned his own concept of the spirit world.

"It's not out there," he whispered. "It's in me. The world of spirits is my memory— I am the world of spirits!"

Why was he surprised? He had searched for the meaning of life and death, the knowledge that was the bedrock of so many cultures, the truths written in esoteric gospels, a faith held in the human heart since the beginning of time.

He had known this all along. One of his characters, an old woman on her deathbed, had told a child, "I will live as long as you remember me. I live in your memory."

So many of the characters in his stories had come to the same conclusion. The departed lived in the memory of the living.

"Everything exists in memory," he said to himself, realizing there was no turning back. "The entire universe exists in my memory! That's all there is!"

This was the way of the shaman, the road he had often traveled to his subconscious, and the road back. It had taken a lifetime to get to this truth. Even God's memory could reside within him.

Letting go meant she was freeing his memory, not leaving— just creating space in his world of remembrances. The angel's gift was bearing fruit.

He would always remember, but he also knew that huge chunks

of memory had disappeared from his mind's storehouse. Like calving blocks of ice breaking loose from the mother glacier and returning to the sea, leaving behind only the memory of ice.

Only glimpses of the past remained. It was natural, the brain's hard drive had capacity limits.

When he was young, the old man had been invited to lecture in Europe. She accompanied him. Wonderful trips, interesting people, fascinating places, exotic food, sensory experiences that had been stored in memory. But of that lifetime only a few images remained.

Why?

The faces of friends he and his wife knew in Paris, Bordeaux, Madrid, Florence, Lisbon, Heidelberg, Mexico City, friends who had often visited them in New Mexico, now fading.

Egypt. He remembered brief images. Riding a camel at the pyramids in Giza, the Valley of the Kings, the Nile, the temple at Karnak. In Paris, Notre Dame, the rose window, streets, cafés, the Eiffel Tower lit up at night. Saint-Malo, Cuernavaca, Mazatlán, Spain, Greece— images all running together, all fading.

Perhaps forgetting was not a cruel game played by nature. Maybe it was nature's gift to the mind. The mind was vast, and the many memories stored therein were more than that powerful computer could store. The mind needed rest, and so it began to erase memories.

It began to let go.

A gift from Mother Nature. Yes.

Every living second of life once resided in memory, even the dream world was stored there, but there was too much material to keep forever. To keep the organism in balance, some old memories had to be erased. The mind needed space to grow into new memories.

Mind, like flesh, needed harmony to survive. Mind was embedded in flesh.

He had tried too hard to contact her in the spirit world, and all along that world was within.

Like a bank full of gold coins, he thought, memories had to be spent for the organism to thrive.

Like it or not, memories piled upon memories and got tangled up. Millions of images, stories to tell the grandkids if one could remember. Like millions of circuits in a huge mainframe, powering down, protein plaque gumming up the wires. There was no rebooting. Neurons shorting out, like a mess of silicon chips gone wild.

Was there an eternal, fixed, unchanging memory?

Men wrote stories and claimed the visions came from God's memory. The new age was into having conversations with God, inviting him to morning coffee for a chat. But any fool could compose stories. Any fool could talk to himself.

"Like me," the old man whispered.

Still, some deep-seated memories begged to be remembered. A memory suddenly appeared: There you are in Granada, walking down a gypsy street, holding her hand, so in love in that exotic place. The gypsy girls came clamoring, begging for money, so you tossed them coins . . . Remember?

But that's it. The million other details of the stroll through the gypsy quarter of Granada were gone. Erased.

We made love in Granada, city of love, streets of love. After an afternoon in the Alhambra we hurried to our hotel. We made love— didn't we? We must have. We always made love in those foreign places.

Remember Granada? Remember how our bodies throbbed under the Spanish sun? The rhythm of castanets, el grito hondo? City of love, blood on the sand of the arena, blood on the hands of the matador— remember?

The old man grew sad. He was confusing the streets of Granada with those in Madrid, Barcelona, León, Valencia . . .

"I don't remember," he said.

He bowed his head and softly repeated, "I don't remember."

Ghosts in the Bush

The old man was thinking.

Am I selfish? A shell fish? A tiny spark locked up in an oyster shell. Ossified. Calcified.

Is the soul a pearl within? How do I describe it?

Is soul mind, and is mind soul?

He looked at his legs. A recent bruise. The legs of old men and old women were often spotted black and blue. Old people fell a lot.

One of the old gals at the senior citizen center had shown up limping, bruises on her shins. "What happened?" her comadres asked. "Nada," she said. "I was making tortillas, that's all."

They knew a falling tortilla doesn't make bruises. Later she confided in her friends. "I get dizzy sometimes, you know."

Yes, they knew. They worried. "Comadre, you have to be careful."

Careful? Didn't matter how careful an old person was, the legs got weak, dizzy spells came on, a throw rug slipped underfoot.

One old fart bragged about his accident. "I was chasing Sadie in bed. Fell off and broke my hip! Ha, ha."

"Yeah, right," his friends laughed, but worry lines crossed their brows. They knew statistics were against them. Hip fractures were a dime a dozen.

The old man told no one about his falls. Two that could have killed him. Maybe his angel's hands held him up, and he wasn't hurt. Only bruised.

"Be careful," they whispered to each other.

"Cuídate," friends said in parting. Take care. Be safe.

Living alone had its dangers. Physical and mental. Who could he call when he felt sad? He didn't want to bother his niece and her husband; they already did enough. His caregivers.

"I'm good," he answered to all inquiries.

It's difficult to share emotions, the old man thought. Emotions rise from memories, and there are too many memories in the world. Stack them up and they weigh more than god-zillion tons. More than twenty moons.

He sang, "Many moons have come and gone since you wandered from your home . . ."

Millions have lost their soul mates. Presidents and thieves, the rich and the poor, the famous and the low. Those who lost a spouse often created rituals around death and grieving. Some heard voices, saw the departed appear in their dreams, thought of reincarnation, heard angels calling, followed the religion of loss, attended the Catholic mass for the dead— candles, incense, prayers.

Did anyone answer grief's prayers?

Grief was spread out across the world like an old blanket wet with tears. If someone could bottle all the grief in the world the stuff would make even Jesus cry.

Mourning became the old man. Deep in his soul he knew he wasn't alone. His lady friend had lost her husband. They had loss in common, and the emotions that came with loss. They exchanged memories from past lives.

But it was time to engage life, and from that struggle, to create new remembrances. His wife had told him that.

Everyone handles grief in his or her own way, thought the old man. You give up thinking and you die. As long as we dream, we live. Grief is a dead weight in the heart. Pesar, the Spanish word for grief. Pesar also meant to weigh something. Grief weighs a ton, the weight of loss.

The old man, seeking a new path toward love, asked his lady friend, "Is it possible to love again?"

The images of their lost ones loomed over the bed. There had to be a letting go.

"Yes," she answered. She was willing to move on. "I went crazy when he died, but I kept it to myself. One day I said enough was enough."

That's what the old man felt. He had to let go. But how could he if his Beloved lived in him?

All over the world women were grieving. They had lost those they loved to wars, famine, ethnic cleansing, misguided revolutions, rape, abuse. Mothers felt the hurt the most. They knew intimately that suffering came with cycles of birth and death.

Nature said, I'll make you tough, woman, because life ain't gonna be easy.

Been looking at this too much from the man's point of view, the old man thought. Got to move closer to a woman's perspective. How would his wife be handling his death if he had died first? A steady hand, he was sure. Much steadier than his.

Those grieving felt connected to others in the same boat. Networks developed. Like wounded fish floundering in a dying ocean, they found each other. Those who could went on cruises together, assisted living homes for the elderly. They read books like *The Seven Steps of Grieving*. One followed the chapters and found relief at the end.

"Bullshit," the old man said.

He was thinking. The mind is the dynamo of the flesh— trust yourself. Transcend.

I am not selfish. I've helped the family, raised a grandkid, given to my community, helped friends. I feel connected to world affairs, vote for just causes, write letters, speak out, lend a hand.

He knew he was arguing with himself. What he had done belonged to yesterday. Everything he had experienced in life now existed only in memory. And could past phenomena be trusted if it came to reside only in a storage bin in the brain? So many random thoughts. The brain hardened with plaque, the mind forgot, memories died.

Who would remember his wife? Her daughters, grandchildren, friends . . . but eventually their memories, too, would pass away.

Her face in photographs, videos, letters, and her name writ in books might last a bit longer, but in the end everything vanished.

When he died, strangers would come to the estate sale, pay a few bucks for mementos that were once cherished. His rocking chair, a favorite painting, a bowl from Zia Pueblo, all his books . . . everything would be dispersed, disappear.

Books held memories! But even books were frail containers of all that had been. Books recorded only snippets of what actually took place. Reality could not be contained— as quickly as it appeared it was swept away by the flood of time. Reality—the fleeting second between the past and the future that some optimists call the present—is an illusion.

All books are fictions anyway, approximations. The old man knew. He wrote books, hoping to encode reality. The entire world was writing books, or making digital videos to put on the Internet. Seeking immortality in a world moving at the speed of light. Eventually everything crumbled to dust.

Electronic messages disappeared into cyberspace. Computer files got erased, the hard drive of the heart crashed.

"Sooner or later we all get deleted," the old man whispered.

Before e-mail, handwritten or typewritten letters recorded a history of what had been. Letters lasted— even yellowed and rumpled, they lasted generations. Now it was electronic mail, and social networks— the new dynamos of power and revolution. Too much information floating through space, creating an unstable history easily deleted by hackers.

Life in the age of too much information was fleeting. Generations came and went, lost, and by the wind grieved. But once upon a time, if you kept grandma's letter you felt connected to her time and some sense of stability. Electronic letters? The old man didn't know where those went.

Ghosts.

Ghosts everywhere. But once, they were real. Ghost from his childhood.

The old man had grown up on the banks of the Pecos River, that river of childhood magic that ran down from the Sangre de Cristo Mountains to empty into the Rio Grande. His river. The river that ran through his soul. "I loved the river."

A river of purity where we fished and swam with friends. We tramped for miles up and down the river. We became one with the essence of water and wind moaning in the trees. But at night the spirits of the river came out. We stayed away at night.

He remembered that's where he first encountered the ghosts in the bush, the spirits that inhabited the river forest. Late one evening his father had sent him to cut wild grass for the milk cow. A cold, dark wind came screaming down the valley— the tall cottonwood trees crashed against each other, tormented by the restless wind.

A dark cloud without silver lining covered the moon. The boy shivered and hurried to the water's edge where the green grass grew thick. Tree branches slapped at him, and he thought of turning back. A piercing cry made him stop. Looking up, he saw a demon woman descending on him.

He knew it was the Crying Woman, she who haunts the river at night. He had been warned.

"La Llorona!" he cried, but before he could run she swooped down on him and yanked his hair. He screamed, dropped everything, and ran. He didn't remember how he got home, but hours later his mother found him hiding under his bed, still shaking with fear. He had felt terror, something ancient in the blood unlike anything he had ever felt before.

"La Llorona!" he cried in his mother's arms. "I saw her! Don't make me go, don't make me go!"

She comforted him, and while she washed the cuts on his face and scalp she told him the story of the Crying Woman. A young woman had been left alone in the world. In a fit of depression she took her children to the river and drowned them. Everyone knew the story.

"Is she real?" the boy asked. His mother shrugged and continued telling the woman's terrible deed.

"When the young woman realized what she had done, she went along the river searching for her children. She became La Llorona, the Crying Woman. We hear her cries at night."

"Is she real?" the boy wanted to know.

"She's a creature in stories told by our people. Don't be afraid."

Still, his mother's gaze lingered on the finger-like scratches on his neck. What had the child really seen?

The boy knew the Crying Woman lived at the river. His parents had told him the story. Stay away from dangerous places or La Llorona will get you. Obey your parents. The story was a warning to disobedient children.

"Is she real or only a story?" the boy insisted.

What could the mother say? These folktales that originated in Spain and later in Mexico were the inheritance of New Mexicans, a way to entertain and teach values to the children. Were the stories real? If they lived in the imagination, they must be real. Like heaven imagined must be real.

"Say your prayers and go to sleep," she finally said.

I wasn't satisfied, the old man thought. Was La Llorona real? What did I see? Who grabbed my hair?

After three days and nights of agonizing, the boy decided to go to the river and confront the Crying Woman. If she was a ghost, he would know; if she was real, she would drown him. To ease his torment he had to take the risk.

Late one evening he slipped out of the house and headed for the river. A tempest was brewing in the west, pushing a cold wind down the river valley.

All was deserted on the barren slope leading down to the river. The last of the swallows had disappeared, and now bats fluttered across the brooding sky. An owl cried, a coyote answered then disappeared in the dark.

The boy arrived at the edge of the river forest and stopped. The darkness was a curtain he would have to part and enter. Could he?

I have to know, he told himself.

Quaking with fear, he entered the foreboding forest and walked quickly to the spot where he had met La Llorona. Overhead, towering trees swayed like giant specters. Screeching sounds filled the dank air. He had entered the abode of ghosts.

"Come out!" he shouted, challenging them, his words a thin cry in the overwhelming cacophony of night sounds. Whipped by the cold wind, trees cried mournfully, and out of the dark night ghosts rushed down to punish the arrogant boy.

My heart was pounding, the old man remembered. I wet my pants.

"I'm not afraid!" he cried.

The Crying Woman appeared, swooping down on him as she had before, her terrifying figure towering over him. Her long, tangled hair fell to the ground, bony fingers reached out to grab him, her open mouth full of sharp teeth.

He shouted again. "I'm not afraid!" But his cry was smothered by the wind screaming through the trees.

She grabbed me, the old man remembered, and I fought back, pushing her away, freeing myself from her strangling, octopus arms. I looked for her eyes, but there were no eyes, only her wild green hair, black in the night. I tore myself free and realized I had disentangled myself from tree branches. There was no Crying Woman. Her bony fingers were branches, her teeth were only slivers of tree bark glistening in the faint moonlight.

I lay on the ground panting, looking up at the protective canopy of trees swaying in the wind, listening to the soft sound of the river flowing by.

The boy had entered the domain of ghosts and learned that the sounds and apparitions of the river were its soul, alive but not threatening. He had become one with the presence of the river. There was no Crying Woman, no ghosts in the bush, just him in the natural world. He was not set apart from nature, he lived and breathed *in* it.

As a grown man he understood that being at the river that night meant he had participated in the earth's consciousness.

As a child he had conquered his fear. The ghosts were only creatures in stories his parents told.

"I was free," the old man remembered. "But sad in a way."

Why sad? Because now he knew ghosts were only creatures in stories. Even angels were just characters in stories. He had followed his fear and found the only things he had to fear were the ghosts his mind conjured up. His imagination reigned supreme.

That was when he began to realize the spirit world was within him.

Now the sadness overwhelmed him again. When he died, the memory of his wife would die with him. Letting go meant acknowledging that memories die.

What of world memory? God's memory. Was there a memory that could provide stability throughout time? Memory in the dark matter that held time and space together. Memory in God. The old man didn't think so.

The ghosts live in the blood, he said. Our human history writ in our cells. Even if there is no eternity that we can trace into the future, we are bound by the past. Connected to ancient memories. We did not come blind into the world. We came laden with the stories of our ancestors, as far back as the beginning of our species. And in that we dwell.

His wife smiled. She wanted to reach out, touch him, and tell him how brave he was. How much she admired him. Yes, it was time for letting go, but as they both knew, they would always be together.

Lovers forever.

She passed her hands over his eyes. Sleep, sweet prince. Of all the stories that live in memory, none are more meaningful than those of lovers.

The old man fell into a deep and peaceful slumber.

She Sees Life

The old man stepped out onto the porch. A half-moon hung in the sky, waxing bright.

"Your moon," he said. Their love had thrived under the moon's cycles. Season piled upon season.

In the garden hummingbirds skimmed the bright red four o'clocks. Morning and late afternoon the seductive flowers bloomed, begging pollination.

Where have all the flowers gone . . . sweet words of love hanging in the air.

Cycles of growth and rest, life and death imprinted into every living thing on earth. This he knew. He trusted nature.

Hummingbirds swarmed at the feeder, sipping sugar water from the glass container, buzzing back and forth, jockeying for position. Notorious fighters.

Since time immemorial, immigrants arriving in New Mexico quickly learned that to survive in the harsh landscape they had to form communities. The arid climate, high mountains, and few rivers dictated that its inhabitants become communal. The communal model prevailed in the Indian pueblos.

"Hummingbirds fight over one feeder," he said. "Not too communal. Why?"

Hummingbird madness, she said.

The old man laughed. "Hummingbird madness. I love it."

But, she cautioned, there's always method in nature.

You're right. We don't know all of nature's secrets. Moon cycles affect these tiny creatures. As soon as October nights begin to freeze they fly hundreds of miles to Mexico. Imagine their little hearts and wings beating all that distance. Like the monarch butterflies. Going south.

She smiled. The beach at Mazatlán. Jemez. Taos.

The favorite places of one lifetime.

Years ago her parents had a home in the Taos mountains. Her father had hung a feeder and dozens of the colorful birds appeared, hovering, threatening each other, zooming, sipping sweet water, then dashing away.

Remember?

Yes.

The Aztecs called their war god the Left-Handed Hummingbird. Carried a war club. Did hummingbirds inspire that?

He thought he heard her laughter, soft as the tinkling of a silver bell around a lamb's neck. Gentle and clear.

On the horizon, the Manzano Mountains stood guarding the pass to Abo. There a gathering of clouds glowed a ripe apricot color. Father Sky held no towering cumulus clouds this afternoon; his arms gently caressed Mother Earth, covering her like a protective lover.

At every turn of the evolving evening, the old man described the scene to his wife. "The clouds of the llano are few and soft this afternoon."

To his words she replied, I see.

He went to sit in the love seat under the grape vines. She sat beside him, as they had so many afternoons in the past, enjoying the panorama, the river's green cottonwood forest, the city spread along the valley, the Sandia Mountains rising into the sky on the eastern horizon, a granite turtle lording over the landscape.

Split tail swallows danced overhead, then appeared the evening bird he loved so well— a nighthawk.

"Glory be," he said. The world is charged with the grace of God. Ineffable.

"I caught this morning's minion . . ." He loved that poem but could only remember the first line. The poems of his youth were slipping away. Also the songs. "I'll write my own!" he said, but knew he would forget those, too. Forgetting was everything. The function of memory was not to remember, but to forget.

He wished he could remember everything she had ever told him. She was wisdom incarnate, a lovely hummingbird who had sipped at the nectar of life, then flown away.

"Many moons have come and gone since you wandered from our home . . ."

The beach at Mazatlán. We loved the beach, made love on the beach. Maybe one day we'll return.

I would like that, she said. Visit all the old familiar places. Gentle sea, vendors on the beach, morning breakfast on the terrace, our favorite restaurants, the mercados.

"Margaritas," he said, and thought he heard her say, Ah, yes.

The ripe fragrance of the tall sunflowers floated in the quiet light. Throughout the hot months the flowers followed the sun's daily path, praising the life-giver, Grandfather Sun.

"Girasol," he said, "turns to face the sun. The sunflower is the face of the sun on earth."

Now the stalks drooped, the round heads bent earth-wise by evening light, gone to dark seed, the once-bright petals shriveled.

Red-breasted finches hung precariously on top of the flowers and leaned over to peck at ripe seeds. So did the small canary-like finches, filling themselves with the bounty of late summer. Evolution at work, perfecting the beaks of different birds as Darwin predicted.

A sparrow cannot be a hummingbird. Don't wish to be what you're not; be yourself. Works for birds and people, the old man thought. But if the sparrow insists it wants sweet nectar from flowers, and it passes those genes on for a million years, eventually sparrows will grow long beaks and learn to hover. Lowly sparrows will become brilliant hummingbirds.

What will the hummingbirds have become in that time?

A fat bumblebee hung on a honeysuckle flower. Honeybees buzzed at the lace and trumpet vines.

That March, standing under the blooming apricot tree, he had listened intently to swarming honeybees, the sound of spring. Now their buzzing at the lace vine announced the changing season.

Hollyhocks dying, then sunflowers. Pear tree changing color.

He remembered the spring, when all was green and tender. The corn's ripe tassels had scattered pollen on the silk. Male and female in one plant.

That morning he had picked a tomato to eat with the egg he fried. The hot summer had been hard on the vines, yet still they gave their fruit.

As a child growing up in the eastern plains of New Mexico, he had watched the nighthawks come up from the river, swooping across the hill. White-banded wings, birds of evening, bringing with them a nostalgia that had filled his heart.

Why did the child feel nostalgia? Why did he cry in wonder at brilliant sunsets? Why these intimations of immortality? Why awe in one so young? Why did the earth wobble beneath his feet?

Because the child would in time become the old man, and no one knows what they will become in time.

Did the Great Mystery know?

Nothing is preordained, he thought. No cycles of reincarnation. Things just are. Then, like seasons, we pass away.

But seasons return. Did the earth's revolutions around the sun create a promise in the mind of early *Homo sapiens*? Nature dies in winter and is resurrected in spring. Maybe that's where we get the idea we will be born again. We died in the last cycle, so we will come alive in this one.

Persephone rising. Jesus rising. The myths of resurrection prevailed.

His life had revolved around his wife, a man of clay feet circling her light, season after season. Then the light expired, her eyes shut down, she died. He lost sight of the promise inherent in the dance they had shared, as if cataracts had enshrouded his will to live.

A ruby-throated hummingbird hovered in front of him, acknowledging his presence, communing for a moment with the old man, then darting away when the dogs approached.

They looked at him, wagging their tails, assuring him, licking his hands. Since the woman who loved them had not returned, they had followed the master's every step.

"I see," the old man said. "She told you to take care of me, didn't she? Yes, that's the way it is. I feel better. Thanks to you and every-one—"

A knot stuck in his throat. He was grateful for family and friends who watched over him. He could not have made the journey alone, this he knew. He had to learn to say "I love you" before it was too late. He loved the saints and he loved the living.

"I love you guys," he said to the dogs.

Love was beginning to be all that was left; perhaps it had always been thus. Had he missed the boat?

The Sandia Mountains glowed a pastel watermelon pink color in the fading light. Watermelon mountains. Some said Sandia really meant Santo día. Saints and kachinas residing in the earth.

The glow comes from the heart of the mountains, he said. Everything has a heart, giving off light and heat. That's love.

Yes, she whispered. That's love.

A faint shade of pink worked its way across the face of the mountains, as if an artist were working magic. Beyond the mountains, the arc of a radiant rainbow over Santa Fe, like the one that had appeared in Troy when Paris showed up with Helen. Summer was the time of rainbows in the land of poco tiempo.

"Mira! El arco iris!"

Some, those chosen, dropped everything and rushed to bathe in the light of God's bridge, from time-bound here to timeless there. Promises to be kept.

"So many evenings we sat here and enjoyed the light. In the wink of an eye our hearts turning—"

He stopped short.

"You see!" he exclaimed.

Yes, I see, she answered.

She was seeing life through his eyes!

The moon, the hummingbirds, the faraway clouds, the dying sunflowers, the nighthawk, the mountains.

She was seeing everything through his eyes, sensing the world fresh as it had been on the first dawn of creation. The mystery unraveling. She had not left him, she was in him! He talked to her, described the world, told her what he saw, and she saw! How could it be? Seeing life through his eyes!

"You've been here all along!"

Yes.

He felt her in him, resting in his heart, in memory. As long as he lived she was in him, enjoying as they had always enjoyed.

"Where?" he asked.

In the rooms I made in your heart. When you rest, I rest. In the Room of Loneliness, I sit by you. When you're happy and full of life, I go with you. When you walk in the park and you tell me what you see, I walk by your side.

Ah, he thought, a peaceful feeling descending on him. You're too much.

We are, she said. Something we learned during this time of transition.

Yes. A time of transition.

Time for a new phase, she said.

What?

Learn to love again.

"Love," he whispered.

In the descending dusk the face of the mountains turned dark blue. He thought of the woman he had met. They had grown intimate. Might he have a second chance at life?

"Is it possible?" he asked.

Yes. Don't waste the time you have left.

The old man sighed. She was in him, he in her. It had not ended.

He felt like a drink. Why not? She had just revealed one more facet of life's mystery. Lovers don't die, they remain eternal.

He went into the house and called his lady friend. Could she come to dinner, share a glass of wine? There were things he wanted to tell her about this strange journey he was on, how love could conquer grief. And he wanted to know how she had lived through her loss, her journey. Everyone on a journey. Who knows, sharing and caring might turn into love.

The Cloud People

Something was raining from the sky.

God's grace. God's love.

The old man sat on the porch, lost in the wonder of the July clouds. For days, exploding white cumulus had been rising over the Sandia and Manzano mountains. Huge, exploding masses of moisture filling the blue New Mexico sky, boiling higher and higher until they stood like giants over the landscape.

These were the Cloud People.

Sacred beings with thick shoulders and giant heads covered with white feathers, war bonnets. They rose, wearing dark skirts with fringes of blue that would fall as rain.

They came as a chorus, singing, rattling gourds, stepping lively. From a holy place they came.

We are coming, from a holy place we come.

We are coming, from a holy place we come.

Over there, the Sky World.

Nature's grace swept the tumbling clouds high into the blue bowl of sky. There, one towering cloud met the vault of the stratosphere, and the top flattened out, creating an anvil shape, a familiar sight that filled New Mexicans with hope.

The rainy season had come at last to the land of poco tiempo. Monsoon, the weather people proclaimed. High and low pressure systems pushing across the vast deserts and mountains of the Greater Southwest, choreographing its weather.

The tug of war between these huge systems drew moisture and energy from the south. Sounds and aromas from Mexico arrived with the dark thunderstorms that raced across the parched earth, then the rain fell, the desert drank, mountains sighed with relief.

That winter he had written every day, taking time from work to celebrate Christmas with family. Trees and presents, a necklace for his lady friend, traditional New Mexican dishes, posole and bizcochitos, farolitos on Christmas Eve, luminarias lit after midnight mass at Taos Pueblo, deer dances at Jemez, a plethora of rekindled joy.

Singing we come.

Singing we come.

From a holy place we come.

The old man's positive attitude continued into spring in spite of the strong winds that flared across the land. His niece delivered his groceries, her husband came and planted a garden. Hope sprang eternal.

From a holy place they come, the old man thought, and gave thanks for them— caregivers.

Summer arrived dry as the shell of a dead cicada. A drought tightened its grip, destructive fires spread across the face of the land, the earth lay dying.

"Rain," the old man whispered. He prayed for rain. He listened intently and he sniffed the air, his dry nostrils seeking any sign of humidity.

Then the Cloud People appeared, down from the mountain, the echo from their drums a thunder that shook the earth, friction from their feet creating lightning bolts that split open the sky.

The old man thanked the Cloud People. He stepped into the garden and rain splashed down on him. The old man was drunk with joy. He danced, hobbling about until a fiery, crashing thunderbolt made him hurry back inside.

"Damn!" he cried. "Did you see that!"

Only those born and bred in desert landscapes know what it means to love clouds. God's grace. A blessing from the Cloud People, the other world of the sky.

Realm of my Beloved, thought the old man. The important thing is to offer prayers of thanksgiving. New Mexicans are multi-cultural, multi-religious, multi-lingual, but all give thanks for rain.

Grace was the purity of rain falling, quenching the thirst in every plant and creature. The tensions created by months of heat and dust finally lifted, summer rains eased the hearts and bodies of the natives. A gentle love blossomed again.

In the corn fields the corn mothers received the tassel-pollen, and their daughters awakened and clung to the stock.

Such were the seasons in the land of measureless time, the land of poco tiempo, as the cabrón gringo had called it.

The old man mentioned the Cloud People to his lady friend.

"It's my inheritance," he said. "Puro indio."

You see—

"During feast days in the Indian pueblos, the men wear rattles strapped around their waists. Dry turtle shells with pebbles inside. As they dance the rattles make the sound of falling rain. Turtles and snakes are water creatures. The Cloud People fill rivers and lakes with rain so the creatures they love can thrive."

"Rain for corn and chile," his lady friend said.

Her father had planted acres of chile, the soul food of New Mexicans. She had grown up among the furrows, hoeing, turning acequia water down the rows. Her body held the aroma of wet earth and green chile plants.

The woman was full of grace.

Maybe her father, visiting the pueblos long ago heard the songs, the chorus of old men singing, the steady drum beat, the sound of thunder on mountain heights.

The grandfathers of nuevo mexicanos had once moved easily among the Pueblo people. Many had taken inditas for wives, created a new community of mestizos, and learned that nature is sacred. But those truths were being forgotten in the land of many changes. Evolution had arrived with its technology and new languages. Freedom, some said. A new oppression, others countered.

Cultural legacy was important and many fought to keep it.

In this land of grace, all was prayer. The whooshing blue skirts of the Cloud People came brushing the earth as they raced down the mountains into valleys of corn.

Corn, chile, tomato vines, squash, orchards, green vegetables, the plants drank, animals drank, rivers rose— relief at last.

The clouds were alive with potential, as was every particle in the heavens and throughout. Out there, in the farthest universe where nebulae danced, dark matter was the rain of the universe, a glue that held galaxies together.

But in the land of New Mexico where the old man dwelt, some said the landscape determines— from the southern Chihuahuan desert to the northern Sangre de Cristo mountains, all is rugged beauty cut by God's rough hands. Or by the goddess, Mother Nature.

From the eastern llanos where the golden carp languidly swims in the Pecos River, moving west to the sluggish, muddy Rio Grande, and on to the Continental Divide, this precious earth embraces the traveler, welcomes the weary pilgrim seeking solace.

The tribes of this region reflect the color of the land. Their blood, like the water that irrigates their fields of corn and chile, is rich with minerals. Springtime floods wash down fertile earth, the mineral-rich river water is turned into acequias that irrigate rows of green crops, and the earth gives its bounty.

In their dances the people praise the spirits of the place. In deep dreams they, too, give thanks for rain, give thanks to the Cloud People.

So it has been for millennia. Such is the power of the Cloud People and their love of this earth.

The old man breathed air tinged with the fragrance of rain and wet earth. He thanked the Cloud People for deliverance. He praised God's grace.

The old man said, In this land blessed by gods, all prayer is one. Prayer doesn't dissolve into separate parts, it clings to the whole, creating a faith that endures. Perhaps in this mystery and beauty unfolding before my eyes there is a small bit of grace for me.

There is, she said.

He turned to face her. I was dreaming.

You are a dreamer, she whispered.

In this land of poco tiempo?

Yes.

You know everything.

I know you.

Poco tiempo. Little time left. Is that it?

Yes, she said. Time measured by the seasons. Maybe later you'll get a whiff of eternity, but don't let that concern you now. Move on. Little time left. Carpe diem.

I told my lady friend—

Be kind and caring, his wife replied.

I thought one love in a lifetime was enough.

She scowled and said, Bullshit. Love is too big to be contained. It belongs to everyone. Go on.

The old man laughed and sat upright. Time to move on?

Yes. Many raindrops make a storm, many loves a lifetime. Get out there.

The old man nodded. You were always full of grace.

That's the way we loved, she said. Don't let it die.

The old man thought he was going to cry. There was just too much beauty in what she said, too much beauty in sky and clouds and mystery.

Yes. A time to live in grace. With beauty all around us.

He got up and went to the phone.

Memoria

A memory cannot be erased. That's what he thought, because once an event had been burned into the brain, hardwired into the cells, it's stored in the brain's hard drive, creating a home in neuron fibers, a constellation of energy waiting to explode into consciousness.

Memories lie as remembrances in dormant cells. Memories store life's narrative, records of a past that will never be again, thus the tragedy of the species. Only memory can dredge up past experiences that have evaporated into space-time. Dreams can do this, but dreams are often hectic, coded in postmodern narrative, Hecate's domain.

Psychologists say they can help the dreamer put the pieces of a dream together, but they're only prompting the dreamer to create a story from dream images. That's fair. The fevered mind's stories offer catharsis.

There are times of joy stored in memory, small rewards. And there's the archetypal memory, the symbols of ancient mythologies stored in the cells. We have all dreamed we were drowning, or dreamed of a dragon, or that we died and rose to heaven, and the most recent image— that of a nuclear cloud that destroys humanity.

Can a person erase a memory? the old man asked himself.

Try forgetting, and tomorrow or five or ten or thirty years down the road the forgotten memory will jump out at you. Some scent or sight, dream or nightmare will trigger the hidden memory and suddenly it's there, a burning image thought forgotten. The brain is an ancient organ.

The old man was reading, seeking understanding. The dogs lay sleeping. Earlier that morning they had chased a squirrel, enough joy to last all day.

Neuroscientists had discovered that memory makes its home in a group of brain cells and synaptic fibers called the engram. That's where memories are stored. The same neuro guys could inject special proteins into the engram and delete a particular memory. Stimulate the engram, a specific bunch of neurons, and you get rid of the information written in it. Memory deleted.

The old man read on. They could move brain cells around and strengthen regions in the brain. They were thinking of injecting a protein called CREB into a specific area of the brain to try to cure Alzheimer's disease. A smart shot! Damn!

Suppose a soldier returned from Iraq or Afghanistan traumatized and disabled by fearful combat memories. CREB could wipe out his particular fear, and the man could lead a useful life again.

Neurons injected with CREB might also help produce long-term memory. Great for remembering events from the past.

Not bad, thought the old man. Science prevails. But I don't want memories of my Beloved erased.

Of course the ancient Greeks were the original memory doctors. In their mythology, Mneme was the muse of memory, daughter of Uranus and Gaea. She played a role in Greek history, as did her sisters: Aoide, muse of song, and Melete, muse of meditation.

Three wise daughters.

There has to be a fourth muse, the old man thought. The muse of forgetfulness.

Or was the muse of grief the fourth daughter?

Memories, songs, and meditation could bring on grief. Listen to Mexican or country western love songs and tears will flow.

"Estoy en el rincón de una cantina . . ."

The old man called his muse, Memoria. She could be a goddess or a bitch, depending on the memories she dredged up. Memoria led the old man by the nose, now here, now there. Remembering is her favorite tactic.

She is a trickster, like Coyote from Native stories, and she loves to take the forlorn on roller coaster rides. Up to the heights or down to despair, she doesn't care. She lives in the heart, not in the brain. Emotion is her sister.

Memoria lies in wait in the engram and when one least expects, she whispers, Remember . . . And emotions flow.

To survive the ups and downs of life, nature gave women an extra dose of adaptability. When a man pulled his hair and cursed the gods, as the old Greeks were wont to do when tragedy struck, the woman picked up the kids and moved on. A higher calling, the old man guessed.

What is the body but a bundle of wired energy driven by brain and spinal cord? The old man read on, trying to keep his head above water. Eventually plaque coats over brain cells, so memories stored therein are boxed in. Proteins gum up brain cells and memories are forgotten. Natural processes.

He thought that understanding the role of memory would help him in his struggle with grief, but grief seemed to be never ending. He was still talking to his wife, memories kept surfacing. He couldn't shut them off.

Last night he dreamed he held her in his arms. A lovely dream. Was she calling him? Was it time?

I miss you, he said daily. Hourly. At every turn, she was in him, it was that simple. He loved her more than ever.

He knew that alcoholics can recover. Even drug addicts can be helped. There are places to go for help, groups where you tell your story, therapies, helping hands, counselors, psychiatrists.

Some human behaviors can be modified, maybe erased. But memories? Maybe. Regression crept in. Thought he had gotten stronger, could go on alone, then his eyes would fill with tears, sadness suddenly there. Grief placed an arm around the old man and together they walked in the garden.

"I'm a wimp," he whispered. "Why bother anyone with this stuff?" Hadn't she said get a life, get out, find joy?

He thought of moving out of the house. Move to Ana's home in Cuernavaca where they had spent so many wonderful summers.

Would running solve his regressions? But Ana was dead, the house sold, the kind maids gone, the dogs gone, the garden, all gone, changed. Memories lived there, too.

Or move back to his hometown, rent an apartment, walk the old byways. Why? Everything was different. The river he had known as a child had been dammed, the summer floods controlled, the house where he grew up had burned to the ground, no trace left, old landmarks changed.

What one saw as a child is not what one would see as an old man. He knew.

Seemed like the entire universe was composed of memories. God's memory. The Great Mystery. Is that it?

He told himself he lived in the present, carried on, took care of things. He had invited his lady friend on a weekend trip to Santa Fe. Had his nephew do maintenance at the mountain cabin, paid his bills, kept up communications with family and friends.

Was it all a game?

Was she calling him?

Not my time, he thought. But he felt fatigued. He bought vitamins and got a new prescription for his sciatica. Bought a bottle of high-priced wine, tried to smile more, flirted with a couple of the old gals at the senior center.

It didn't work. He couldn't commit. He felt he had little to offer. Where was the joy he had once known?

Fits of depression still came around. Family and friends visited, but mostly he was alone. He attended a few events, but always hurried back home. He lived in a deep silence. Afternoons he spent staring at cloud-laden skies. Was he thinking too much? Living too much with memories?

Fear of going crazy returned at times. He thought of the day he would die, arranged the will, began to give away things. A sure sign of preparation.

Was he moving on? When? Where?

A Divine Dream

She appeared in a dream, standing near him, clear as life.

Did she come with a message? When he awoke he felt excited, thankful to have seen her. So real he could have touched her.

It wasn't until he was eating breakfast that he looked at her photograph and wondered aloud, "Did you come for me?"

Was that it? She hadn't said anything in the dream, just stood by him, a divine presence.

"I'm not ready," he said. His response surprised him. "I have to finish the story I'm writing, granddaughter's baby is due soon, income tax time, spring cleaning—"

He stopped short. He had promised to be with his Beloved sooner or later, so why wasn't he ready? The nostalgia he had felt as a child came over him. A sense of going home, the true home that could only be with her.

Surely the mundane things he had to do were not important enough to keep him from her. Had he found a purpose in life? Or was it that no matter how sick the body, it just didn't want to die?

Should he bother with the garden? Why plant anything if he wasn't going to be around to taste the fruit? Was he getting ready? Did old people at the right time feel this sense of letting go? Is that why at some point they just gave up?

"I'm not ready," he said again. "With luck, I can live another five or ten years."

Did he want to?

He thought of joining a counseling group so he could ask others if they knew this feeling— like dying. He didn't mention it to his doctor. What could he say? Doc, I feel like I'm dying.

Dumb.

He had been writing friends letters, just to stay in touch. Some he hadn't seen in years. Was this a sign of getting ready?

Too many questions. Dreams, like memories, could be disturbing. Without the right interpretation, they could create psychological worry or worse, fear. Imbalance. Body and soul needed harmony to thrive.

Anyway, the real world was within. This he knew. He didn't believe in divine intervention. Not from outside forces. The divine was within, this much he had learned. Experience was the teacher, and the important thing was to participate in the here and now.

If anyone was divine, she was. Were dreams the only way to know the divine? Devils and monsters also arrived in dreams. Shadows from the ancient caves. Blood memory.

Memories. He was back to that, more confident now. Memories constructed the mythology of the soul. He could trust in that.

She was divine intervention, messenger and message. He felt comforted. She had come for him, but was he ready? He didn't know.

Who can plan to be ready? Nobody. A split second is all it takes for a heart attack, a stroke, an accident, and suddenly the living are left behind. But the living are connected to the departed, he knew.

He was growing stronger, and letting go didn't seem so fearful anymore.

"Ay, mihita," he said, slurping down the milk in his cereal bowl, reaching for the cup of strong coffee that was a god-sent elixir in the morning. "In memory or in dream, you are in me. Take my hand whenever . . ."

A resolution.

He walked into the garden, the dogs at his side. He looked up at the rising clouds. A low pressure system in the eastern llano had pushed a large cloud bank over the peak of the mountain.

"Clouds rising today," he said.

Good, she answered.

"Beautiful day. Maybe we can go for a walk later. Go to the pond, see the fish. Flocks of geese going north, following the river. Nature on the move."

As always, she said. Plant a garden. Nothing better than home-grown tomatoes.

He listened. She was right.

"Yes. Like always! Why not!"

She encouraged him, pushing him across the fertile garden soil so he could smell the earth, reach down, pick up handfuls of compost, and let the mystery of regeneration run through his fingers.

Hope springs eternal! See the clouds!

The old man looked at the rising Cloud People. If there was resurrection, it lay in the mystery of sky and earth.

A new awareness hit him, sweet as her kiss. "I'm seeing through your eyes!" he exclaimed.

He looked around and realized he was seeing what she saw. It wasn't just him telling her what he was experiencing; she, too, had been pointing him in the right direction. Mystery of mysteries.

"What now?" he asked.

Love, she answered as she walked down the hollyhock path.

Are you leaving? he asked.

I go to prepare a bed, she replied, blending into the dazzling sunlight that was so bright it made the old man dizzy.

"Bendito sea Dios," he whispered. She walks in beauty, with beauty all around.

The dogs came to lick his hands. "You saw," he said. "Been seeing all along. I'm just slow. Okay, home-grown tomatoes it is."

His nephew had cleaned the yard, turned the soil, gotten everything spring-ready.

Don't know what I'd do without family, the old man thought, and gave silent thanks. Need to tell them I love them. In the meantime, no moping around!

He looked to where she had disappeared in bright sunlight. A streaming rainbow rose up to the gathering clouds.

So much to be thankful for.

Daughters bringing dinner tonight. Meatloaf and baked potatoes, a bottle of red wine, ice cream for dessert. Later, I'll watch my tele-novela. Wish I could write a tele in Spanish. Nuevo mexicano ancestral Spanish, mixing in Spanglish, English, barrio slang I learned from the pachucos in the fifties, a real tossed salad.

You could, he heard her say. She had no doubts.

They had met one summer in a literature class at the university, and it was love at first sight. He saw it in her eyes. Thereafter he would see the same love every time he looked at her.

You caught me, he liked to tease her.

We were meant to be, she answered without skipping a beat.

Yes, he agreed. It couldn't have been otherwise.

He sat at the kitchen table and leafed through his journal, the details of their life together, random entries, a jumbled narrative.

He adjusted his glasses and read. We met one summer in a literature class at the university. Svelte, the word that best described her. Slender. A lithe spirit, two or three inches shorter than me, a seductive walk. I immediately felt a tug, her gravity.

He took a pencil and erased. He would need a thousand and one nights to really describe her beauty. He had tried, but he wasn't pleased. From time to time he erased entries or tore out pages. He thought photographs told a better story than his descriptions. She had class.

Her eyes. Magical bright eyes.

Something in the glances we exchanged gave me the courage to invite her for coffee at the student union after class. The coffee got cold while we talked for hours. I kept looking into her eyes. It was love at first sight.

A cliché, he thought. Should he erase the entry? No, it was love. Love came from the heart through the windows of the soul. Why deny it? Something burst loose in me.

The old man paused and laughed. Damn, did I write that? What a romantic. It was true. She was a beauty. More than that, she was regal, patrician. Words, words, words.

I went home moon-struck. Began to write her love poems. The budding poet. Is that what it was? Love does engender poetry. I was no poet, but I wrote.

"I want to read everything you've written," she told me. She was inspiration divine.

She was perfect, not angelic— a woman.

She told me she had two daughters. That didn't cool my feelings. Right then I thought I could do anything! She floats on earth. We made love. A perfect fit.

He turned the pages.

A tumultuous summer. Proposed, got papers ready, finally did it. She is tender, loving.

He had made a list of early trips.

Guaymas, the beginning of our romance with Mexico. The beach. She tans a soft brown, a moist skin. Is skin where passion begins? Loves the sun. Her sweat tastes like sea salt. Yellowstone, Great Salt Lake. Bobbing in the water. Short trips at first . . . Wish I had kept a travel journal.

She read my stories, thinks they're great. She teaches lit and drama, has a sharp eye for editing. I don't like critical comments, but yes from her.

Took a lot of adjusting to get used to family life. Did I fit? Without her love, care, and determination, things might have fallen apart.

I tried to define true love. How did our love come to be? I remember a story. A silly anecdote, but interesting. In the beginning, man and woman were one person joined at the belly button. God took a knife and split them apart. Now and forever after, each man goes searching for the woman whose belly button fits his. Each woman searches for the man whose belly button fits hers.

Don't know where I heard the story, but when the belly buttons fit, that's true love. Ours fit. I am a romantic. Belly buttons reunited. I should write a story based on this dumb tale.

Maybe not so dumb . . .

Love is doing and caring for the other. She cared for me. Oh, yes. Rubbed my sore shoulders, was attentive in every way. In her hands lies the art of healing. So many more of those small details I need to write. But for whom?

Note: If Eve was created from Adam, then she didn't have a belly button. She came from a rib, not her mother's womb.

There goes the belly button metaphor.

Travel. Paris. We walked out of a café one evening after dinner with Jean and Denise— they took us around the corner and surprise! There shone the Eiffel Tower in all her glory. We stood in awe, holding hands. Jean got us a taxi to Vincennes. I guess he told the taxi to take the river route. The Seine at night, us a couple of innocents abroad from New Mexico in the back seat . . . How much more romantic could an evening be?

Love is giving. She gave, and I was on the receiving end. The drive from Trois-Rivières to Quebec City one October. From there to Boston.

I forgot a lot of those events. Times in New York, conferences. True love was difficult to put into words. Let the poets write the passage. Love just is. You'll know.

The old man put the journal aside. He felt tired. He was spending too much time writing. Daydreaming.

"We were meant to be," he said to dispel the sadness creeping in.

He knew the only way out of an existential crisis was to get going. That meant caring for family, community, and the poor of the world. Care for the earth, mother of all. Not to receive, but to give, as long as he could.

There are many divine dreams in the life of an old man. This was one. There would be many more.

Clouds

The old man was dreaming.

He sat rocking, covered by the immense, immutable, blue-bowl vault of sky. He dwelt in the center of a circle— around him, three hundred sixty degrees of horizon. Where sky touched earth was but a frail line; no one knew its color.

Horizon was an illusion. Was it earth touching sky, or sky touching earth? When lovers make love they are indistinguishable.

The old man looked at the rising clouds. Sky determines old age, he thought. God's abode.

All seasons instill wonder in the people who dwell in the land of the pueblos, but this was the summer of the old man's content. The west wind blew in towering rainclouds from the western shore. This wind is a trickster. Plan a picnic when weather reporters predict all will be calm, and Brother Wind will come roaring in right when the paper plates are on the table.

Praise the wind.

A southern wind, this source of life wind, brought tropical air from Mexico and the gulf, a moisture-laden atmosphere. When these two winds met, they gave birth to huge cumulus clouds that filled the bowl, exploding with life-energy until the entire sky became a brimming of spirits.

The Cloud People came to bless the earth.

From the west they are coming.

From the south they are coming.

The holy people come.

The old man sat on the porch, releasing his thoughts to the wonder of the thing. Like all who take time to contemplate the beauty of clouds, he felt awe-struck. Beauty seeped into his soul, a human wonder so immense he gave silent thanks.

The firmament touched him and spoke its secret: I am the Great Mystery.

The old man accepted. It was all he knew.

Billowing white clouds, like giant gray-blue whales splashing across a sea-sky, leaving in their tide dark downpours that rained across the face of the Sandia Mountains. Turtleback Mountain, a water creature frozen in granite, rejoiced. Rain at last.

Lightning bolts flashed fiercely, like rattlesnakes striking across the vast space, crashing, thrashing, piercing the earth with their magnetic electricity, releasing ozone, a love-fragrance. In this realm of the sacred, lightning flashes opened the womb of clouds, and sky's orgasm gave forth rain.

The water of the woman is like rain from the sky. Lovers know this truth.

A rainbow arched in iris beauty, a bridge that gathered the four corners of the land in its embrace. The profane ran to look for pots of gold. Others simply said, Gracias a Dios.

The dogs sitting by the old man whined. Their ancient nature stirred with the approaching storm.

In the garden, the satisfying roll of thunder shook the sunflowers, whose large, pregnant heads drooped with seed.

The Cloud People come, the old man whispered to his wife.

Yes, she said. Your universe has always been animated.

The old man nodded.

The clouds rose and grew like white mushrooms with dark underbellies, spilling their dark pollen on dreamers and lovers. In the bosom of the Great Spirit, the Cloud People took shape, kachina spirits in flowing skirts, Rain People. They stirred the breeze that rolled across the valley, refreshing the faces of city workers on the way home.

The calm before the storm gave way to tumult— to chanting, gourds rattling like the sound of falling rain.

The Cloud People came, down from the mountain they came, dancing they came, stamping their feet they came, lifting their mighty bodies, growing so tall and powerful the entire sky-bowl was soon filled with their dance of promise.

Already it was raining in different segments of the horizon. Over toward Belen and north toward Santa Fe, dark clouds blessed the earth. The Cloud People filled the sky from Taos to Las Cruces, from Gallup to Santa Rosa.

Four sacred directions sped away from the center of the Zia Sun, light divine. Realm of the sacred, realm of the profane. Flesh and soul, so it was. So it has always been, for it is fallen Adam who must sing songs of praise to the rain givers.

The earth, sanctified, breathed relief, like a woman just filled with sperm, her yearning complete in the arms of her lover.

The Great Mystery. This is all the people know.

The Cloud People rained on the earth of the ancestors. The earth drank, lovers groaned, love satisfied.

Remember? she teased.

The old man smiled. I remember. Thunderstorms were always a time to make love. Here and in Mexico. Rain falling on the tile roof at Ana's home in Cuernavaca. Spain, Egypt, wherever.

He heard her soft laughter, like the first drops of rain.

Rain comes and we inhale God, the old man said. I have often wondered, why here? Why so much beauty in this land? Why here in New Mexico where the struggle has been so long and difficult? Harsh land and poverty breaking our backs. Is this our recompense?

Yes! Look! Listen! Smell! Fresh aromas in the breeze, mountain pine fragrances, silk of corn plants, earth sanctified, rainbow of unicorns! Our recompense!

Fractal geometry could measure the clouds, but could math measure the spirit within? The last poets on earth were struggling with the spirit of a restless god. A god so terrible he gave these moments of beauty to the old man, and let children in Somalia starve.

Beauty and truth is all we know. Follow your fear, he said.

Wondrous advances in science, medicine's apogee, body parts for the old, come one come all. Most of the old man's friends now wore new body parts. Why not?

Science could not answer spirit. All was within the soul, not in the technology. Incredible change had come to the land of the ancestors, and so many would have to follow their fear. Would they find answers in the dark abyss?

His ancestors had come and stayed to raise crops in the land of the pueblos. We worked hard, the old ones said. Our backs broke and our hands were stained with blood. But one afternoon lived beneath this sky provides enough beauty to fill our souls for another day's toil. The earth provided, the sky rewarded.

They propagated, raised children with the same care that they raised corn, babies born the color of earth, the color of yellow, red, and white corn. Umbilical cords of the just-born, recently cut from still-bleeding ombligos, the color of red earth. Cries of promise resounded in adobe homes. Placentas buried in corn fields, whatever the weather.

That's what the old man heard, cries of the newborn in the fresh wind rising.

The Great Mystery loomed over him, immutable, indifferent, unknowing of the beauty it created and the emotions it roused in the old man's heart.

What awful power brought the clouds to the land of New Mexico? How did we come to dwell in this land?

So many stories tried to answer these questions. Was there a power beyond the clouds? Did some foreign god reign over the clouds? The stories of the world described sky gods, from Zeus to Jesus, ascending.

For the old man, living in the miracle of the Great Mystery this afternoon was enough. More than enough, fulfillment.

From time immemorial, tribes had composed stories of the gods beyond, earth-shaking, sky-determining gods. Beautiful stories from down the generations: epics, visions, esoteric gospels written in parched leather, rich tomes, bibles to lift the spirits of those poor of heart. Stories upon stories, so many a man couldn't read them all in a lifetime. Since the beginning of the species, the tribes had prayed to gods beyond the clouds.

The old man had read many of the far-ranging stories. But this afternoon sitting on the porch under a cloud-filled sky, he was satisfied to whisper, "The Great Mystery is all."

For this miracle in which I live and thrive, even as an old man, I give thanks. Old age has its recompense.

He felt her near. His wife, his Beloved.

"You," he whispered. "Where?"

Here, she replied.

A cloud descended in front of the old man. A cloud in the shape of a bed, wondrous and lovely, golden with light and rainbow colors, a bed befitting Pallas Athena in her Olympic rest. A bed large enough to hold the passion of Christ, the love of the Virgin, the mystery of death.

"Ah," the old man sighed. Mystery of mysteries.

Was he dreaming, or had he awakened into a larger dream?

His wife, in a rainbowed flowing gown, stepped out of golden sunlit clouds and reclined on the bed.

Come, she beckoned. It's time to rest.

Yes, he said, smiling, exhaling a breath of satisfaction, contentment at last.

You promised, he said.

I kept my promise, she replied.

The old man left his rocking chair and began to climb up the cloud to the top. He had climbed the cliffs of Jemez in his youth, and now he felt as agile and strong. He went, eager to be with her, pulling himself up until he lay beside her.

I'm so glad to see you, he said.

It's time, she answered, and fluffed his pillow as she was wont to do in a past life.

This is like heaven, he said.

Love is heaven, she whispered, and lay her arm across his body.

The feathery cloud rolled south, carrying the lovers across a sparkling rainbow and into the arms of the Great Mystery.

Before he fell asleep, the old man spoke.

"I thank God for bringing me this far. I thank my ancestors for leading me on the right path. Thank my wife who dwells with me. Thank the Great Mystery for this cloud-studded sky. I bless those I loved and now must leave behind."

He closed his eyes and slept, and the cloud carried the lovers south to Mexico and over the beach at Mazatlán. The aroma of fresh-cut mangoes greeted the lovers, as did the calls of vendors on the beach. Many other wonderful sights appeared and disappeared as the cloud continued on to the land of the Maya.

The cloud would circle the earth— such is the mystery of clouds. The old man and his wife would sleep. Maybe one day the cloud would return to the land of New Mexico, where once dwelt these two lovers.

Also by Rudolfo Anaya

Bless Me, Ultima
Heart of Aztlan
Tortuga
The Silence of the Llano
The Legend of La Llorona
The Adventures of Juan Chicaspatas
A Chicano in China
Lord of the Dawn: The Legend of Quetzalcóatl
Alburquerque
The Anaya Reader
Zia Summer
Jalamanta: A Message from the Desert
Rio Grande Fall
Shaman Winter
Serafina's Stories
Jemez Spring
Curse of the ChupaCabra
The Man Who Could Fly and Other Stories
ChupaCabra and the Roswell UFO
The Essays
Randy Lopez Goes Home
Billy the Kid and Other Plays

Children's Books

The Farolitos of Christmas: A New Mexico Christmas Story
Farolitos for Abuelo
My Land Sings: Stories from the Rio Grande
Elegy on the Death of César Chávez
Roadrunner's Dance
The Santero's Miracle
The First Tortilla
Juan and the Jackalope: A Children's Book in Verse
La Llorona, the Crying Woman
How Hollyhocks Came to New Mexico